W9-BRE-382

PRIMAVERA

by Mary Jane Beaufrand

LITTLE, BROWN AND COMPANY
New York ⁓ Boston

~⊙~

Little, Brown and Company

Hachette Book Group USA
237 Park Avenue, New York, NY 10017
Visit our Web site at www.lb-teens.com

First Edition: March 2008

The characters and events portrayed in this book are
fictitious. Any similarity to real persons, living or dead,
is coincidental and not intended by the author.

ISBN-13: 978-0-316-01644-5
ISBN-10: 0-316-01644-6

10 9 8 7 6 5 4 3 2 1

RRD-C

Printed in the United States of America

The text was set in Bembo, and the display type is Aeneas Light

To the real Emilio
In Memoriam

Prologue

Florence, 1482

I am forging a gold ring one spring morning when Signor Botticelli comes into our shop. I slouch closer to the anvil and draw my tunic tighter around my neck. I pray he does not recognize me. Indeed, my disguise is good, and it has been four years since we last met. Besides, Signor Botticelli only notices beautiful things. I am not beautiful, with my face smeared with ash and smoke, my hair bound up in a rag. I look like what I have become: a goldsmith's apprentice.

He coughs dramatically and brings a kerchief to his nose. It must be a shock for customers to go from open air to our tiny inferno of a workshop, always stoked and hot. It must be like entering hell.

My master greets our guest warmly, wiping his blackened hand on his heavy apron before extending it. "Signor Botticelli, I am pleased to see you. How many years has it been? No matter, no matter, you are most welcome here."

Signor Botticelli bows low, his hawklike eyes darting around our cramped shop. They rest on me briefly but then turn to something else.

As he and my master speak I allow myself to take in the rest of him. The four years have been kinder to him than to me. His sandy hair is streaked with gray; his garb is that of a rich man. His cloak is lush green velvet embroidered with tiny flowers. It looks as though he is wearing an entire meadow on his back. Underneath his cloak rests a heavy gold cross with one single ruby embedded in its middle, and etched swirls like maiden's hair winging out to its four sides.

The cross is my handiwork. I recognize it at once.

"Maestro Orazio," Signor Botticelli says formally. "It is good to see you as well. But I must tell you I am here on business. I am the bearer of glad news and a commission."

"Of course, of course," my master says. "Come take a seat here, away from the fires. Maria! Bring our guest some wine, if you please." He shouts to his wife who is upstairs, making the bread for our midday meal. Our living quarters are as small as the shop and just as smoky. I don't mind the smoke anymore. I breathe it more easily than air. Some days I feel like Vulcan — an ugly monster making beautiful things for spiteful gods.

Signor Botticelli sits on the wooden bench by the window and loosens his cloak. Underneath he carries a delicate dagger strapped to his tunic. I can see the workmanship on the hilt — an ornate floral design, also my own. At one time in my life I would not have noticed the workmanship at all. Just the sharpness of the blade.

My master sits next to him, leaning back in practiced ease. He wants it to seem as though the two of them are equal. But they are not. Anyone can see that. My master is fat from Signora Maria's cooking. His paunch strains his apron strings. The few teeth left in his head are black. Everything about his person declares that he is nothing: a mere tradesman in a town of rich, embroidered men.

"What brings you here, Signor Botticelli?" he asks.

"I came to tell you that my patroness has word that two weeks ago the villain Girolamo Riorio, Lord of Imola and Forli, was apprehended and summarily executed as befits his crimes."

At his news I feel my face redden. I know who his patroness is. We all do; even though we dare not mention her name. She is Lucrezia de Medici, mother of Lorenzo de Medici, the one we call *Il Magnifico*. She is also the mother of Giuliano, who was stabbed to death during Easter mass at the *duomo* four years ago.

So Count Riorio has been caught at last.

Signora Maria appears with some wine in a skin jug and a large sausage. She is a round woman in middle age, red-faced like the rest of us. The sausage she brings is so fresh it smells of pig. The meat was to have been part of my keep, but I do not begrudge our guest this extravagance. *Eat well and begone,* I will him.

Maria, on hearing the news about Count Riorio, begins to cross herself, then stops with her fingers over her left breast. She is a pious woman and would pray for the soul of even the most hardened criminal. Still, she should save her pity for above stairs. Showing pity for the wrong person in Florence is dangerous. Soldiers still drag bodies through the streets, although, *Grazie a Dio,* lately of no one I know.

Signora Maria rushes from the room muttering something about unbaked bread.

Maestro Orazio spits at his feet, trying to cover his wife's indiscretion. "Good riddance," he says. "Death is too kind a fate for that assassin."

"Indeed," agrees Signor Botticelli. "My patroness still grieves for her murdered son although he has been cold in the ground these four years."

"Perhaps this will ease her burden a little," suggests Maestro Orazio, nervously wiping his hands on his apron.

"Perhaps," Signor Botticelli agrees. "She is of the mind that this is the last villain of the Pazzi Conspiracy. She has persuaded *Il Magnifico* to put this matter to rest. He has stopped pursuing the Pazzis. As well he should. They are all dead or imprisoned. They are no threat to the Medici anymore."

Signor Botticelli does not look at me as he says these words. He does not give any indication that he recognizes me.

And yet his words give him away. How long has he known?

I look again to his cross and his dagger. They are his only pieces of metal and they are both of my making. Could he have been spying on me all this time? No; that would be too strange. My fear is making me imagine things.

"Basta," Signor Botticelli says, taking a long drink of Signora Maria's heavy, sedimented wine. He was always overfond of drink. "Enough news. Now the commission. I require a ring. You know the size. It would please my patroness to have the design of a dove on the lid. The dove should be of inlaid stone."

My master nods knowingly. This is our specialty. We make the rings with compartments. I know exactly where to put the hinge so it will be unnoticeable but easily unlatched in haste; say, to dump the contents in a bowl of soup.

Signor Botticelli draws a small leather sack from his cloak and hands it to Maestro Orazio. When he catches it, it jingles like a pile of coins. A big pile. "She would like this done in haste. You will deliver it to me and not to her directly. A week from Sunday, midday at my studio."

"Your patroness is a generous woman," my master says, not pausing to count the coins in the sack, although I know he is itching to do just that. "You may be assured of my quality and discretion."

"I knew I could," says Signor Botticelli, taking one last swig of wine before getting to his feet.

Then, to my horror, he points directly at me.

"That youth over there," he says. "He has a circumspect face. You will send the ring with him."

"Emilio? He is a sullen lad. But you are correct, sir. He is discreet. I vouch for him personally." Maestro Orazio pretends jocularity, but his words, like his smile, are tight.

Signor Botticelli pauses at the open door as he puts his cloak back on. A breeze is blowing, sending in welcome, clean air from the hills above our town.

"Remember," he says one last time, fixing me with his steady gaze. "Next Sunday. Midday."

As he leaves I allow myself to inhale deeply of the fresh air. Is that rosemary that comes in on the wind?

Emilio, Signor Botticelli called me. *Youth,* he called me. In truth I am neither. Of late the masquerade has grown difficult. For a while I tried to hide my figure under layers of clothing but was forced to stop the practice when a loose sleeve caught fire. Now I slouch behind something large. This anvil, for example.

I set the hot ring down and inspect my hands. They are black. Underneath the black is red from the constant heat; underneath the red is the fine, white cross-hatching of scars which have made a tapestry of my palms. I know I shouldn't, but I like the layering of colors. Three layers, each different. What would you see if you cut me open to the heart?

A host of good memories comes back to me with the scent of open air. There was a time when my hands, like my life, had just one layer. I remember sparring with Emilio — the real Emilio — in the courtyard of my father's palace. I remember my nonna sitting in the family kitchen, peeling an orange in the soft firelight, her long hair the color of ash coming free from her cap.

Now, back in the shop, I wipe my face with my hands, suddenly sick. I should have known that if I allowed in the good memories, the bad ones would come back as well: the strong scent of almonds, the sound of an earthen pitcher crashing to the floor, and the sight of my sister Domenica running through the house, tearing her hair, wailing, "Now we can never get married!" I remember that was the worst fate she could think of. Even then I knew that what had just happened, and what was about to happen to us all, was far worse.

Maestro Orazio shuts the door and the scent is gone; the memories along with it. Once again the shop smells of fire and smoke.

I tell myself I am better this way, shut up in this hot cell of an existence, never going out, never even looking up. It is too late. The shape of my life has already been etched on me, just as deeply as the marks on my skin.

As I put the ring back in the fire I turn my head to the window and allow myself to look outside.

For a moment, just a moment, I had thought it might be spring.

Chapter One

I t was early 1478 when my family's fortunes ebbed, like the waters of the Arno. Those who still speak of the April Rebellion say how sudden it was, how no one had any idea things were so bad in our city of flowers. But I say there were clues. Those who didn't see them were men like *Il Magnifico,* who only listened to good news, never noticing shadows gathering around them until it was almost too late.

Me? I saw the shadows, or at least I thought I did. But what did I really see? Just bits and pieces, pretty words whispered through half-open doors by men in dark cloaks.

There was only one person who tried, really tried, to open my eyes to what was going on around me. *You think this a game?* he had said, pointing from a rooftop. *Look. Listen. People pass by your window every day whose lives are nothing but toil without respite. You live but two blocks from the Bargello prison yet you don't hear the screams of men who have forgotten everything pretty.*

I did look. But I didn't see. And for that I am no better than the rest of my clan. Worse, in fact. For what did I do to the boy who tried to open my eyes, the one who I now know I loved better than all others? He is dead. All that remains of him is rotted black flesh over bone. And I am the one who killed him.

The year was 1478. My name was Lorenza Pazzi, but everyone called me Flora. I had eleven brothers and sisters. I was the last daughter in my father's house.

Now, there are days when I feel I am just the last.

∽◉∾

"Are you sure, Flora? We have twenty-two diamonds and not twenty-three?" my brother Andrea asked. We were in the courtyard of my father's *palazzo* on a warm spring afternoon — the first of the season. I was on my knees, scraping the soil around rose bushes that the tender roots might breathe better.

Andrea sat by the gurgling fountain with a ledger open on his lap. We had spent the morning inventorying the items in my father's bank — pearls and silks from the Orient; golden table services from princes with good taste but not good sense; ancient marble statues of gods long forgotten.

"Yes, Andrea, I'm sure," I said, running my fingers

through loamy earth. Around me was a sea of moss, lush and soft as fur — a perfect antidote to being locked inside an airless chamber and counting gems and musty tapestries.

He shook his head and closed the ledger. "All right," he said. "If you say twenty-two, twenty-two it is. There can only be one conclusion: Francesco is stealing from us."

"What?" Francesco was my father's best worker, someone who had risen from a position as manager of the family's silk business in Genova. He was an honest soul who savored numbers as others might delicate dishes flavored with rosemary. I knew he wouldn't even think about shorting us one small diamond. One small diamond with a flaw at that.

I knew because the stone was hidden up my sleeve. *I* was the thief, although I didn't tell Andrea.

"It must be Francesco. There's no one else."

I tried to stay calm. "What will you do?" I asked.

"We'll have to let him go." He shrugged.

"*Per favore,* Andrea. Let him stay. Francesco is a good man. There must be another explanation."

My brother closed the ledger and got to his feet. I couldn't help noticing that he looked a bit shabby. His tunic was velvet but the colors had faded; his stockings had been darned and darned again until his legs looked as though they were woven in place by giant spiders.

Andrea was a logical man. Until last winter he'd been studying at the University of Pisa, where his specialty was dead languages and dropping things from the leaning tower to see how fast they'd fall. But then Papa summoned him back to help run the family businesses. He probably liked Andrea's plainness of dress and manner as much as I did. With Andrea, I rarely found myself thinking what he *really* meant, as I did with the rest of my family and our courtiers.

"*Bene,*" he sighed. "I won't put his name forward to Papa. But Flora: this can't continue. With the new Medici taxes, we need every florin we have."

After he left to go upstairs to Papa's study, I crossed myself and thanked God that, even though He had plunked me in the middle of this greedy family, He sent me at least one good relative. Two, counting Nonna. As for the rest? My eldest sisters were all married before I turned fourteen — mostly to other merchants who were willing to swap money for our pedigree. They seemed lovely and docile enough until you got to know them. They reminded me of species from myth who would sing to unsuspecting sailors only to dash their brains against sharp rocks.

And my brothers? Conniving toads, to a man. Even Antonio and Lionardo, who had taken orders and were now in charge of bishoprics in San Gimignano and Perugia, had eyes that narrowed with greed. I watched them all parade through the courtyard and up the stairs to my father's study, their eyes darting about, staying too close to my father's fortune and their inheritance.

But I had little to do with them. When I was fourteen

they were gone from the house. The only four of us left were Renato, my eldest brother; Domenica, my older sister and the beauty of the family; and Andrea.

And where did I fit in with this clan? I was not beautiful, like Domenica; I was not practiced in flattery, like Renato; nor was I learned, like my brother Andrea. While the others had their *sprezzatura,* their effortless mastery, I had none. I was just Flora. I lived to help other things grow.

After Andrea left, I stayed in my garden cultivating thorny shoots. A youth from my father's guard came in the front entrance carrying a letter. He wore the tunic with the family crest — the Pazzi dolphin — but he wore it ill. Underneath it he looked thin as a bundle of twigs.

"Excuse me, *signorina,*" he said, bowing deeply. I glanced around for Domenica. His manners were so courtly; he must have been looking for her. But there was no one else. This boy must be new. The rest of the guards didn't bother being formal. They usually said: "Hey, Flora, give this letter to your father." Or, more often, and with a glint in their eye: "Give this letter to your sister."

This twiggy boy looked ill indeed. His cheekbones were sunken and the skin around his eyes was black-blue. Flies buzzed around the velvet *mazzochio* on his head, which also fit so loosely it looked to be unraveling. His belly was distended, as though he had been very hungry and then eaten a large feast. Since I listened to my nonna when she talked about vapors and humors, I knew what was wrong with him. He had been eating the cook's rancid, mealy black bread.

"You can puke if you want to," I said, pointing to a potted orange tree.

He raised his head and looked into my eyes for the first time, as if trying to decide if I were joking. Then he dropped a letter, ran the length of the courtyard, and vomited into a delicate white container.

Poverino. He heaved even when there was nothing left to bring up.

I picked up the letter he'd dropped. I read my papa's name, Jacopo Pazzi, in elaborately gilded script. I turned it over to examine the seal. Neatly embedded blood-red wax was the mark of *Il Papa* himself, Sixtus IV. The pope had written to my father.

"That's for Signor Jacopo," the boy said. "It's not womanly to open it."

"It's all right. I'm not womanly. I'm going to the convent."

"Oh," he said, looking relieved. "They told me that one of the daughters was in the courtyard so I assumed . . ."

"That I was the pretty one?"

He nodded silently.

I liked this boy. He was honest even when he was sick.

"What do you know about Marco Polo?" I asked.

He looked thrown off balance by my question, as was I. Why

did that even come out of my mouth? All he did was puke in the orange tree and I handed him the content of my dreams.

The youth stared at me overlong, taking my measure. "Not much," he said finally. "Only that when he first returned from his travels no one believed him. They say he stood on the altar at San Marco in Venice, slit open his robes, and a king's ransom in jewels fell out."

This youth didn't know it yet, but he said exactly the right thing. Because here is what I hid from Andrea along with the flawed diamond up my sleeve. Mamma said I was too plain to marry so she gave my dowry to Our Lady of Fiesole. I didn't want to go. I couldn't stand the thought of spending the rest of my life indoors, growing wrinkled and blind from sewing someone's undergarments in dim light. It was only by the grace of God and the intervention of my beloved nonna that I wasn't there already. But Nonna was old and could not live forever, no matter how much I willed it. One day she would leave me. I was determined that when that day came, it would finally be my turn. I would take my stolen gems and use them to buy my way to Venice, where I would book passage on a ship to the Holy Lands, battle infidels, and rescue the bones of some saint. From there I would ride on a camel through the mountains and have tea with a Chinese lord with a moustache so long it dragged in the ground. When I came back, I would stand at the altar during high mass at our *duomo*. I would slit open my robes as Marco Polo did, and say: *See, Papa? Is this enough? Do you love me now?*

He would embrace me in front of the whole city. He would tell me he loved me and that he always knew my true worth. I would never have to tend anything again.

"What is your name?" I asked the youth in front of me.

He looked at me kindly, and the shadow of a smile crossed his face. "Emilio," he said.

"Well, Emilio, I'm Flora. I'll show you to my father's study, then you will come with me to the kitchen where we will get you some real food. None of that black bread they give you in the billet. I've seen what the cook puts into those loaves. Rat droppings and powdered snot."

I pointed my finger down my throat and made gagging noises.

If I thought Emilio's half smile was interesting, his full smile warmed me like the sun. I even liked his two crooked front teeth.

"What shall I do about the orange tree, eh?" he asked.

"Leave it," I said. "She'll get over it."

I didn't know why I said *she*. It was my garden after all. But for some reason when I thought of puke in the delicate white vase I thought of Domenica.

Chapter Two

Our *palazzo* had rooms for everything — cooking, sleeping, bathing, reading, plucking, praying. Each space seemed stuffed more than decorated. There was no corner without a bust; no wall without a painting or tapestry. Mamma said that the Medici were smart enough to patronize artists so we must do the same or we would look coarse. We did everything the Medici did.

I led Emilio up the marble stairs to the *piano nobile* — the floor where all the activity in the house took place. The stairs brought us directly into the great hall where my family and their minions ate their evening meal around a large U-shaped table. I rarely was invited to sit with them. Mamma said I was too plain for good company and that I honored my family best by serving the meals and then dining in the kitchen where I would be more "comfortable."

I called Mamma a wench sometimes when she wasn't listening.

Today, Emilio walked two paces behind me through the Madonna gallery to Papa's library. The *poverino* was swaying so hard I feared he would fall over, and his eyes seemed to spiral in their sockets as he looked from side to side. All those enthroned virgins crammed into that long, narrow space. Don't get me wrong — the paintings and busts were all lovely, but there were too many of them. They made me dizzy; I could only imagine how Emilio felt.

At the end of the Madonna gallery the library door was ajar, so we stood at the threshold and had a good view of half the room. I stood back and motioned to Emilio to stand behind me. I was good at peering through half-open doors.

My father was within and pacing, his soft leather shoes padding quietly on Carrera marble.

My mother, who was closeted with him, made a lot of noise. I glimpsed the elaborate black and tan brocade of her gown as she swished from place to place. The timbre of her voice was high and reedy and pierced my skull.

I turned to Emilio and put a finger to my lips. We weren't spying, exactly . . . well yes, we were. But we were doing it through an open door. God would forgive us.

"But think what an alliance would mean, Jacopo," my mother said.

"We already have one, Maddelena. My brother married a Medici."

"That is different," Mamma continued. "Guglielmo married a Medici *daughter*. You know as well as I that daughters mean nothing."

I cringed. Mamma told me this daily with looks and sharp words, but I'd never heard her lump all the daughters of the world together. After all, Domenica was a daughter too.

Mamma continued: "The power lies with the sons. Lorenzo would have been a better match. Still, Giuliano would be a fine son-in-law. And, God forbid, should something happen to Lorenzo, your daughter would be First Lady of Florence."

Giuliano was Lorenzo de Medici's younger brother. Lorenzo was already married to a Roman girl and they had two sons. Giuliano would not inherit the bulk of the family fortune, but he was still rich and powerful enough to please my mother.

My father pounded his fist on the desk. "Medici, Medici, Medici. I am tired of hearing about those wool merchants. Who do they think they are, anyway? My ancestors were out defending the Holy Land when those upstarts were still guarding sheep."

That was a common rant of my father's. *What right do they*

have to be richer than we are? They do not wear crowns. They have never even been knighted, like we have. They are mere peasants.

Mere peasants with enough business sense to finance a pope. Mere peasants who rule our city as if they were kings. For all their humble beginnings they must have done something right.

"I'm not saying we have to *like* them, Jacopo," Mamma said. "But think of the power we would wield. More votes would go your way in the *Signoria*. They would be forced to accept us as equals."

The *Signoria* was the council of leading citizens of Florence. They decided on civic issues (taxes, levies, maintenance of common paths) based on a ballot of stones — red stones for yes, black stones for no. They voted in the open in front of all the other important men. There was once a time when measures my father proposed all met with red stones.

Now, too often, his proposals met with black.

I heard my father sigh; then watched his silhouette drop in his chair. He seemed heavy with fatigue. On top of the black votes and the sleepless nights, he was weighed down by my mother. She weighed us all down. "All right then, Maddelena," he said. "What do you propose?"

"Giuliano has seen Domenica Sundays at mass and thought her comely. We must do all in our power to make her even more comely. She will need more dresses and jewelry and a maid of her own."

"More dresses? Why should she need more dresses? She already has three," Papa said.

"Variety, Jacopo. In order for a woman to get a man's attention she must seem to be many women. Do you remember when we were courting? I wore a different dress to each mass then. As I recall, you thought well of me."

"I thought well of your money," he muttered.

Mamma kept talking as though she hadn't heard his barb. "We must have her portrait painted and present it to the Medici. The portrait must show Domenica even more lovely than she is in life."

I saw where this was going. I groaned softly and rolled my eyes. Emilio looked at me, confused.

My father understood. "Please," he begged. "No more Madonnas."

"Why not?" Mamma pleaded. "Our daughter is certainly beautiful enough to rival the Queen of Heaven."

I held my breath. Next to me, Emilio crossed himself. This talk of my mother's was not good. Mortals couldn't talk like this without inviting serious consequences.

I drew breath again, surprised we hadn't been struck by lightning. But now I was even more afraid. My mother wrought something with her words. I hoped we would not all have to pay.

My father seemed to give up. "And you already have someone in mind," he said.

"Lucrezia de Medici prefers to patronize the artist Alessandro Filipepi — the one who calls himself Botticelli. He will do nicely, I think."

Lucrezia's husband, "Piero the Gouty," had died young and she'd lived more than half her life as a widow. Lucrezia didn't seem to mind. Without him, she could boss her children about all she liked. I'm sure most days my own mamma wished Papa would contract a bad case of gout.

In the library, Papa sighed. "I take it this Botticelli is expensive."

"Moderately so, I believe."

"All right then. Do what you need to do. This is not my province."

I knew by my father's words that he was done. I rapped on the door as though we'd just arrived.

My mother opened the door wide. She was even more startling up close than she was in silhouette: her black lustrous hair held in a tight knot by alabaster combs, her elegant gown spanning the width of the hall. But the bump on the middle of her nose — the one that no amount of white powder could hide — conspired to make her look coarse.

She looked first at me and then Emilio. She took in my uncombed hair, my ruddy cheeks, my formless shift. Then she sized Emilio up, the too-big clothes, the rank smell, the flies around the cap.

"Why aren't you outside?" she said to me.

"This youth has a message for Papa," I said. "He didn't know the way."

"Bene," she said. "Don't linger." With that, she covered her nose with a handkerchief and pushed past us.

My mother and I were not allies. If I had been Domenica she would have not only spotted my flaws, she would have corrected them. *Come, bambina mia,* she would have said. *Your hair is unkempt and there's a spot on your skirt. I shall have someone fix you up.* Sometimes I longed for this treatment; mostly I was glad she left me alone.

"Flora, what do you want?" my father called.

My father, even indoors, wore a red *mazzochio* on his head that resembled a giant strawberry. He didn't like anyone to know that underneath he was bald.

"This youth has a letter for you, Papa," I said.

I nudged Emilio forward. His hands shook as he held the letter out to my father. Papa grabbed it from him without looking at his face.

Then my father's eyes went wide when he saw the seal.

"Leave me," he said abruptly.

"We'll be in the kitchen if you need Emilio to send a reply."

He waved us away.

"Kitchen, Papa," I said as we left, and I closed the door behind us. Later, after he was done reading and analyzing the letter, he would remember and send for us.

In the meantime Emilio swayed on his feet. He needed to eat and quickly, so I took him to the kitchen and Nonna.

Chapter Three

Now I come to the part of my story it most grieves me to look upon. I have lost everything — my garden, my family, my way of life. I miss Mamma and Papa not at all. I do miss Andrea, but he wasn't like Nonna. Nobody was.

For the first fourteen years of my life Nonna was everything to me. She was my captain, my nurse, my parent, my cook. She was possibly the ugliest part of the *palazzo* — stooped and toothless and surly like a pasha — but the way she dispensed care and comfort made her beautiful.

And now once again I am walking down the back stairs to her realm. Once again I smell the rich odors of sage and thick broth and honeyed bread. Once again I feel it is possible to be made whole.

I cross the threshold of memory and there she is in plain back dress, one long gray braid snaking down her back, moving independently of the rest of her, as if it were always swatting at something. I see the black-dog ring she wore on the middle finger of her right hand, a ring made of gold and onyx that even now I wear around my neck in a chain forged of silver, a reminder that I am a prisoner of regret. Nonna loved me enough to give up everything for me. And even though I loved Nonna, I took her for granted. To me, she was just another part of the house, like the black kettle that simmered on the hearth behind her.

That morning Nonna was hard at work, slapping a loaf into shape. "There you are, you lazy girl," she said when she saw me. "Did you not hear me calling? Come wash your hands. Knead the dough while I finish with the soup."

Behind her were Graziella, the kitchen maid, and two *contadine* braiding garlic. Graziella chopped the heads off a pile of dead rabbits. *Whack!* I didn't trust that girl. *Whack! Whack!* She took too much joy in wielding that cleaver.

Outside the kitchen was a bench full of Nonna's patients. Nonna was an accomplished healer; some even whispered that she was a *strega,* a witch. Either way she was never at a loss for patients. Most brought something to barter for their health: turnips, ducks, rabbits, pine nuts. A few, a very few, came with their hands empty. Nonna never turned anyone away.

Today it was crowded with people who suffered from overindulgence. Lent was almost upon us and most of the town took their forty days of deprivation seriously. So seriously, in fact, that the days before Lent they drank so much red wine they were more poisoned than stupefied. Nonna sent them away with jugs of water seasoned with chamomile flowers. ("The water's the thing," she often told me. "No witchcraft about it.")

I washed my own hands and set to work. "This is Emilio," I said. "He just puked in the oranges. Can you fix him up?"

Emilio, who was standing next to me, stamped on my foot hard. So I elbowed him in the ribs and nearly sent him flying out the door, he was such a stick (albeit a stick with a foul temper).

"Basta!" Nonna said, pulling Emilio over to the daylight. "That is enough, Flora." She was a head shorter than he, but she got right in his face and screwed her right eye up until it resembled a spyglass. "Open your mouth," she commanded.

When she was done, she turned to Graziella and slapped her hard on the face. "What have I told you about using that old meal for bread, eh? These boys work hard. We do not need to poison them."

"But Signor Jacopo told us we should cut costs. I thought to myself: why waste food? Those ruffians should be grateful for what they get," Graziella said.

Emilio was staring at the tops of her breasts, which looked as though they might spill out of her dress at any moment. *Don't pay attention to those,* I wanted to say. *She's a lazy slattern.*

Nonna was still berating her. "If you're smart you'll worry less about Signor Jacopo and more about me. Now go to the pantry and throw out everything with worms in it."

Graziella skulked out of the room. Nonna made Emilio sit on the wooden chair by the hearth and poured him a mug of soup.

"Drink it," she instructed him.

"It's hot, *signora* . . ."

"DRINK IT!"

Emilio gulped it down. I tried not to laugh. It was probably scalding his throat, *poverino.* Nonna's cures were seldom gentle.

At this point my father bellowed down the stairs. "Boy!"

My new friend wiped his mouth on his sleeve and stood up quickly.

"Tranquillo," I told him. "There's no need to rush."

When his eyes met mine they were hard as diamonds. "Maybe *you* don't need to rush," he said. "Some of us have to earn our bread."

He slapped his empty bowl on the table and darted up the stairs.

After he disappeared Nonna stood looking after him. "That is a good boy," she said, "but there is more wrong with him than just his stomach. Perhaps a recent tragedy keeps his humors out of balance. Flora? Are you hearing anything I'm saying?"

I wasn't. I had grabbed a wet dish and a towel and made a big show of drying it, all the while inching closer to the stairs, hoping to overhear what Papa told Emilio. I wanted to know what was in the pope's letter.

"Bah! You listen to all the wrong things," Nonna said as she went outside to tend her patients.

Meanwhile, my father and Emilio stood at the top of the stairs. Papa spoke *sotto voce,* as though he didn't want anyone else to hear. I heard him just fine.

"You will take this letter and ride to Forli," he said. "You will go alone and be quick about it. At Forli, you will deliver this directly to Count Riorio at his court. You are not to give it to anyone but Count Riorio directly. You will not give it to a guard, you will not give it to a courtier, you will most decidedly *not* give it to his wife. Do you understand?"

"Subito, signore," Emilio said, and dashed off to the stables.

I didn't understand. Why was Papa writing to Forli and not Rome? I knew that Count Riorio had married a niece of the pope, but I thought Papa should have sent his response to the Vatican.

I did understand that the pope was different from Papa's circle. In some ways he was like a Medici — a ruler with vast resources who could tax and wage war — but he also had God on his side. One bad move and *poof!* There goes not only your empire but your immortal soul as well.

My father had chosen to tread carefully. By sending for Count Riorio rather than the pope himself, he was asking for advice from someone in the pope's inner circle before posting his reply. A shrewd man, my papa was.

～⊛～

I almost told my sister Domenica about the letter from the pope but thought better of it. During dinner that night I was on my way from the great hall, carrying the carcasses of pheasants stuffed with pine nuts and dates, when she accosted me. She was wearing a gown of silk so delicate it made no noise when she moved. Her face was whitened with lemon juice and goat's-milk paste. She was supposed to look like an angel, but to me she looked like something that crawled from under a potted orange tree after a heavy rain.

She had just been entertaining our company with a song. Her voice was weak, but her face was fair so our male guests seemed willing to overlook her one tepid quality.

"Charming singing," I said. "I liked the one about the coy shepherdess. It made me want to go out and frolic."

"At least you *can* frolic," she said. "I grow tired of being pinched and petted like a piece of livestock. If Signor Turnabuoni pats my rear *affectionately* one more time I swear I'll slap him clear to Milan."

"Oh! Let me!" I said. "I'll slap him!"

Domenica smiled in spite of herself. "Sister, once I am safely married, you may slap whoever you wish. But for now, I need you to give this note to Captain Umberto."

She reached into a pocket and drew out a folded letter, sealed and scented so heavily I thought I might gag.

She waved it in front of me. I was not fast enough to take it. "Quickly now," she said. "Before someone sees."

I did as she said. "I don't like this," I whispered. "Captain Umberto is a good man. It's not right to be trifling with him like this."

Domenica laughed a tight laugh. "You sound like such a *contadina,* Flora. I am not trifling with him. Lots of married women have lovers. I don't see why I should be any different."

It is not fair, I thought as I walked away. She has a banquet of love. Might not a little crumb be spared for me?

Captain Umberto was out front, escorting our guests in and out of carriages. Mamma liked his to be the first face our guests saw, since he was so handsome. He was not in his first youth — experience lined his eyes and face, making them seem carved as though from Carrera marble. And those eyes, *Madonna!* They were warm and lively as firelight. Some days I could hardly bear to look upon him, knowing as I did that he was not for someone like me.

He took the note, unfolded it in front of me, and his features dissolved into a soft smile. "I heard your sister singing earlier," he said. "I wished I could be above stairs with her on nights such as these. Young girls are not livestock to be paraded about so. How fares she?"

I thought: I'd never heard anyone say Domenica couldn't sing in quite so polite a manner.

I told him: "I think you would find yourself in her favor if you could cause Signor Turnabuoni to fall into the muck as you deliver him to his carriage."

Captain Umberto smiled. "That shouldn't be too hard. The man is a drunkard. *Ciao,* Flora. See you tomorrow."

Later that night, after our guests left, I punished myself by leaning over the railing outside my third-floor room to see the two of them embracing by the fountain in the courtyard below. The moon lit up the scene below as plain as day. The garden was scented with jasmine that I had trained around the columns that lined the cloistered walk. What I wouldn't have given to have a moment like that myself, sitting in a moonlit garden on a warm spring night with a handsome man whispering to me, cupping my face in his hands tenderly, admiring me as though I were a work of art.

"Our sister plays a dangerous game," I heard a voice call.

Andrea was also about. He stood on the corner opposite me, holding a goblet of wine from which he sipped. His face had a heavy look to it, as though it might topple forward. My leaning tower of a brother.

"Andrea? Why are you still awake?"

"I could ask the same," he said. "Something on your mind?"

I came close then to telling him everything about the

diamonds. But I didn't. Domenica's secret rendezvous was an open secret; I didn't want mine to be the same.

"Change in weather," I said instead. "Too balmy for me to sleep."

My brother nodded and inhaled deeply. "Tell our sister she should be careful. We can't have the workers whispering about her and Captain Umberto."

"Why? Domenica says lots of married women have lovers."

"Lots of women aren't prospective Medici brides. Lucrezia de Medici misses nothing. Domenica must appear to be more than a girl — she must be perfect in everything she does every minute of the day."

I thought that sounded like a terrible existence. Never getting your hands dirty? Never eating too much? If I had possessed my sister's beauty I would have given up long ago and said I didn't need a Medici. A groom with a smaller fortune would do — preferably one I'd already met and liked.

"If you're so worried," I asked, "why are you up here and not down there breaking them up?"

Andrea sighed. "I know Captain Umberto. He will kiss. He will whisper. Nothing more. Domenica will be clean."

I didn't know exactly what clean meant but knew that it had something to do with the wedding night. It sounded like an ordeal to me, but Andrea used to say it was only an ordeal if you made it so.

"Besides," Andrea continued now. "We all need our little freedoms. Don't we, Flora?"

The night was light enough for me to catch his penetrating glance. He knew. He was waiting for me to confess. And I almost did: a secret of one was just a secret; a secret of two was a conspiracy. And although I liked the idea of having a co-conspirator, in the end I did what I always did: I turned the conversation back to him.

"And you, Andrea? What are your little freedoms?"

Andrea drained the dregs of his wine in one mighty gulp. "Mine have already come and gone, Flora. These days I live to serve."

If Andrea meant to speak with conviction he failed miserably. His words were empty as his jeweled goblet. We were alike, my brother and I, each yearning for something other than what we had. But whereas I still held out hope, he had none.

I drew closer and placed a hand on his arm. "Listen," I said. "In the morning I'll ask Captain Umberto to find us a cannon ball. Then tomorrow night we'll come back here and drop it and you can show me how it falls at the same rate as a feather."

Andrea smiled at me, a rare bud in a city overgrown with tradition.

"I spoke in haste, *cara mia*," he said, kissing me on the forehead; "as long as I have you I will always be free."

After Andrea and I said goodnight I went back into the room I shared with Domenica. I withdrew a black velvet pouch from my pillow. Guided by candlelight, I dumped the contents on my bed. Then I put a hand up my sleeve and took out the small diamond I'd taken from the bank today.

Fourteen small diamonds, one for each year of my life. It was enough to get me to Venice. But would it be enough to book passage on a ship to the Holy Land? I reminded myself to ask Andrea about the cost of working on one of Papa's merchant vessels. Subtly, of course.

I brought each stone up to the candlelight, examining every crack and bubble. Andrea said diamonds were worthless unless they were perfect, but I found perfection boring. It was the flaws that made them beautiful to me, made me long to possess them.

I put the diamonds back in their pouch and replaced the pouch under my pillow. As I did so I counted all the things that my sister had that I would never have: beauty, marriage, the love of a good man, the approval of Mamma and Papa. I pushed my bare toes underneath cold sheets and snuffed out my candle. Then I closed my eyes, tight and still tighter. When I closed them tight enough, I saw the sparkle of sunlight on waves and heard the roar of the sea.

Chapter Four

I spent the next three days in the courtyard preparing the garden for spring. I trained the climbing roses around columns and scrubbed the scum from the fountain. It was filthy work, but I loved it.

At sunset I went to my third-floor balcony, grasped a dip in the roof, and swung myself up. I scrabbled up the steep pitch of the red tiles and situated myself at the zenith, facing north and east. Below, carnival revelers were reeling through the streets clutching their wineskins. There were to be horse races in the Piazza Santa Croce — not as elaborate as the ones in Sienna — but enough to draw a crowd. From where I sat, the people making their way to Santa Croce looked like water pouring through narrow funnels. One man caught sight of me and offered me a necklace of glass beads if I'd show him my breasts. His companion, a man equally drunk, whispered something in his ear. "Sorry, Flora! I thought you were a wench," the first man called. The second man waved. "Tell your nonna we'll see her tomorrow! *Ciao!*" With that, the two of them lumbered off, laughing at some joke.

I told myself I was just trying to get a glimpse of the horse races. It didn't occur to me that I was spying for Emilio, who came the third morning after he left during a moment I wasn't spying for him.

I was in the courtyard on my hands and knees, weeding around stepping stones. I heard a *bang!* as the door to the *piano nobile* was thrust open. Papa came out adjusting his strawberry *mazzochio,* followed by Renato, whose fingers jangled with heavy golden rings, and then Andrea. They didn't linger in the courtyard but went straight to the front of the *palazzo.*

Then Mamma emerged followed by Domenica. Mamma fussed at my sister and drew a veil over her face. They never did that unless they went outside the *palazzo.*

"What's going on, Mamma?"

"Flora, dear, you're wanted in the kitchen," she said coldly, still fussing with Domenica's veil.

"I didn't hear Nonna call me," I said. "If you don't mind I'd rather not waste sunlight." I went back to my plants.

Mamma sighed and turned to face me. "Nothing for it but

to pretend you're a waif. If anyone asks, we hired you to weed the yard. While Riorio is here call me Signora Pazzi." She drew a veil over her face, and she and my sister joined my father in the front.

Riorio. Emilio must be back, then. I looked at my reflection in the fountain. Waif was right. I had my hair in a wrap, but the few strands I could see were clumpy with grease. My face was smeared with dirt, and my hands — *Madonna!* I looked like a *contadina*.

I splashed some water on my face and tried to do something with my hair. I wanted to see our visitors.

I arrived in front in time to see a procession arriving with Emilio in the lead. Behind him were half a dozen men on horseback and one gilded carriage. Emilio himself dismounted and tethered his horse to one of the iron rings we'd drilled into the walls for just this use. The *poverino* looked even more ghostly than before he left. His hands were shaking so hard, he hid them behind his back, awaiting orders that didn't come — the rest of my family was too busy with the man in the carriage, who I assumed was Count Riorio, nephew of the pope.

As my father greeted our guest, I slipped Emilio a freshly picked orange.

"Please, *signorina*," he said, his eyes flicking to my brothers. "Not now."

"If you're worried about eating in front of them, just stand behind me. They won't notice," I whispered.

"I'm a soldier, *signorina,*" he said, holding his chin high. "I don't hide behind anyone's skirts."

But I kept holding the orange out to him, and finally he grabbed it and got behind me.

Meanwhile, I took a good look at our visitors. I did not like what I saw.

To begin with, they were all in black from head to toe. Black boots, black leggings, black tunics, black cloaks. One of them drew his dagger and used it to dig at his nose. He brought away a concoction of nose grit and blood, which he wiped off the blade with his fingers and flicked onto the street.

And their master? I found it hard to believe he was anyone's nephew. His hair under his brown *mazzochio* was already graying. But it wasn't his age so much that struck me as his complete and total pomposity. He had the air of a man who answered to no one. He too wore black: black head wrap, black velvet tunic, heavy gold cross. My father clasped his hand, and I could see that he was half the height of the rest of us. He grasped my father's arm and whispered in his ear . . . *fratello mio*. My brother. He had a smile like slow poison.

Behind me was much tearing and squirting. I craned my neck around to see Emilio finish the last of the orange, peel and all. Nothing was left over. Juice dribbled down his chin and he lapped it up with his tongue and fingers.

"How long since you've last eaten?" I asked, horrified.

"How long since I left?"

He swayed on his feet, and I gripped his hand to steady him. *Madonna!* Between my father and his new snaky friend, they were conspiring to kill this poor wretch. "Swallow your pride," I said. "Andrea!"

Mamma looked my direction and shook her veiled head from side to side. I was supposed to be incognito. Too bad; this was more important. At least I wasn't an embarrassment to my favorite brother, who excused himself and came over.

"What is it, Flora?" he asked in a clipped merchant-like tone.

"With your permission I will take this youth to the kitchen. He has had a long journey."

He shot me a *what should I care?* look.

"From Forli? It isn't but two days' ride."

Then he saw Emilio's state, and his expression changed. "A short ride but a hard one. You have executed your duties well and with due haste. Go now and rest with the knowl-edge that we are pleased." He nodded slightly and went back to the welcoming party.

I took Emilio through the courtyard but didn't get a chance to ask him about the roads because Nonna came out of the kitchen and offered him her arm. He practically col-lapsed on her. He didn't even protest or try to maintain ap-pearances. With me he was a soldier; with her, a little boy.

~◦~

That night at dinner, Andrea called me aside. "I told Captain Umberto that your new swain has done well. The Captain assures me he will take the young man under his wing and that he will make a fine soldier."

"Thank you, Andrea," I said.

We glanced at the dinner party around the U-shaped table. Most finished eating and now Domenica sat in the middle serenading everyone with some tune about love and loss. There were pearls woven into her fair hair that cast subtle rainbows in the firelight.

Riorio's men stood in a group aside from the rest. I was used to men with guarded faces, but these men made even the Medici look open and friendly.

Andrea must have had the same thought. "Look at them," he said. "They are on us like a pestilence."

"I saw that one pick at his nose with his *squarcato* earlier," I said, pointing.

Andrea didn't appear surprised. "Keep your eyes open, Flora. You are in a position to hear more than either Renato or I. Riorio is openly appealing to Papa's vanity. I fear what he will urge our father to do."

"*Bene.* I shall do so. And Andrea: that boy is not my swain. Too scrawny."

Andrea smiled. "Not for long. Did you see the way he tucked into his capon tonight?"

~◈~

The next morning Riorio dealt me my first blow.

When I came downstairs at dawn to labor in my garden,

his shadowy men were in the courtyard, moving statues and digging up flowers and herbs.

One great big oaf of a man crouched over a rosemary bush, yanking at it like a rotten tooth. "What are you doing?" I yelled.

A different man, the one with the nose grit, was moving a potted orange tree into the cloister walk, away from the sun. He brought his fingers up to his chin and flicked them in my direction. *Get lost.*

I grabbed the orange tree from him. "Answer me, blockhead. What are you doing?"

The word *blockhead* got his attention. He did not like to be insulted. Nor, it seemed, did he like having to explain himself to girls. "We have orders, *signorina.*" He spat the last word at me.

"Whose orders?" I asked.

"Your father's, of course."

Around me everyone kept yanking and cutting everything I'd worked so hard to arrange. I felt each blow to these plants in my own shins. I was being torn up.

My father? Order this? I didn't think so.

At this point Captain Umberto came in from the front, shadowed by Emilio, who was looking a bit more robust this morning, although at the moment I didn't care.

"Did you know about this?" I asked the captain. I was not polite.

"*Si,*" he said, ashamed. "Your father says that we are soldiers and we've grown fat. He thinks we need a place to practice war. I had no idea it would be this bad."

"Fine. You want to be a warrior? *Make them stop.* They're not listening to me. You," I called to the giant still whacking the roots of a rosemary bush. "Leave that alone. I need that one."

He also made a rude gesture.

I seized his arm. "I said *stop!*"

He tried to jerk his arm away, but I wouldn't let him. With one hand he pushed me in the chest. I was off balance but grabbed hold of his forearm — the one holding the ax — and sank my teeth into flesh. It tasted like sweat and dirt and ale and stupidity. He yelped and palmed me hard in the nose. I skidded across the sea of moss.

Here is a secret I do not like to share. I was bruised and shaken, but *I liked it.* I liked the exhilaration of my skin being scraped raw. I would get up and do it again, because part of my secret wish was coming true: I was having an adventure. I was battling the infidel.

My progress stopped when I collided with someone's legs.

At the same time, Emilio let loose a wild cry and, his head low, plowed into the man who had pushed me. He sent them both flying into a marble statue of Venus. *Crash!* All three tumbled to the ground. For a skinny guy, Emilio did pretty well.

I rose to my feet, my skin draped with dirt and moss and blood. A hand was offered to me, and I took it.

"*Grazie,*" I said. The one who had offered me his hand

was a little barrel of a man — short and round. His skin was pale and smooth but for little rays of wrinkles around his eyes. He must have been in his thirties. His clothes were vibrant: a bright purple tunic over verdant leggings. There was a feather in his velvet cap. He had sandy blond hair and his eyes seemed to absorb everything around him. Where had he come from? He clearly wasn't a goon.

"Are you all right, *signorina*?" he asked graciously.

Without waiting for an answer, he turned to the men who had paused ripping up my world. "*Cretini!* What are you all doing? Destroying such beauty. You would be whipped like dogs were this my house. Pay no mind to them, *signorina*. We will have you arranged for your sitting in no time." He picked moss out of my hair. "I know your mother commissioned me to paint you as a Madonna, but your beauty is not of a poised quality. Perhaps some personage from Roman myth? Venus to enflame your groom's desire?"

My groom? What was he talking about?

"Flora!" Nonna called me. She stood in the corner of the courtyard, twisting a heavy ring on her finger so violently I was afraid it would spin off her hand and fly to the roof.

Next to me, the face of the man in purple lit up like a thousand torches at the sound of my name. "Of course," he muttered. "Flora."

By the shards of the marble statue, Emilio got to his feet. The giant he took down remained down. Nonna put an arm on my friend's shoulder, inspecting him for cuts and bruises.

She blotted his lip with her apron. "Come by the kitchen when you can and I'll fix you up. And you," she said to Captain Umberto. "Do you think you can keep this vermin from wrecking anything else for an hour? I need to have a word with my son."

Captain Umberto straightened his back. "Of course, Signora Cenesta. You have my word."

"I hope you're ready to back that up," I muttered. He shot me an annoyed look, but I didn't care. I knew he was supposed to be heroic, but he had stood idly by while Riorio's men destroyed the paradise I'd wrought from dirt and a bit of green. Today he was not my hero.

"And as for you," Nonna stepped up to the man in the purple tunic and whiffed his breath. "At least you're not drunk yet."

"I don't know what you're talking about, *signora* . . ."

"Don't start with me, Filipepi." She wagged a finger at him.

I wasn't surprised she knew this man. She'd treated half the city for one ailment or another at some point.

"These days I go by *Botticelli,* Signora Cenesta. Sandro Botticelli."

Botticelli. Of course! The painter Mamma commissioned. Now I understood. He thought I was Domenica. That explained why he was so gracious to me.

"What, your old name wasn't good enough?" Nonna said. "Bah! Your poor mamma. I trust her fever has subsided?"

"Indeed it has," Signor Botticelli answered with a small

bow. "She asked me to thank you for the oranges. And may I congratulate you on your lovely granddaughter, Signora Cenesta? It is easy to see where she gets her beauty . . ."

Nonna whacked me on the back of the head. "Don't wipe your nose on your sleeve. Stand up straight." She turned to Botticelli. "Not this one, *stupido*. You want the empty-headed one. I'll send her down. In the meantime, I don't care how brilliant you are. If I catch so much as a whiff of wine on you before the evening I'll boot your arse back to that smelly goldsmith's. Do we understand each other?"

Signor Botticelli bowed low. "What can I do but obey?"

Nonna fixed him with a piercing stare. "Save your manners for the Medici. We'll have none of your toadying here. Come, Flora. We have an appointment with your father."

As we walked away, I kept looking back to Signor Botticelli in his purple tunic, standing in the ruin of my garden. The sea of moss was gone; the orange trees were gone; the rosemary half-uprooted. I should have been destroyed as well. Instead I watched him as he carefully rescued a tender bud from a pile of roses and placed it on his cloak. I liked that he picked the smallest and most fragile to rescue instead of the largest and most showy. *Here,* I thought, *is a man I would like to know.*

Chapter Five

They say that over one hundred years ago, when Brunelleschi submitted his plan for the giant dome of Santa Maria del Fiore, Cosimo de Medici (grandfather of *Il Magnifico*) said it was too big a thing and it would collapse. He demanded a demonstration. Brunelleschi sent for a raw egg. "If I can make this stand on end, will you believe me?" he countered. Cosimo agreed.

With that, Brunelleschi cracked the bottom. *Half* the egg stood up perfectly.

That day, as Nonna and I burst into Papa's study, I had no doubt as to the architect of my destruction.

Count Riorio was leaning over my father, who was seated

at his desk. Up close I saw that Riorio's face was lightly pock-marked. Without his *mazzochio* his hair was full and gray. He reminded me of some icy creature of the north — a bear or a wolf, maybe. And he looked as though he would have no problem cracking a lot of eggs — beginning with my father's bald head.

"What have you done to Flora's garden?" Nonna bellowed.

In the corner, Renato and Andrea jumped.

"Mamma," Papa nodded, his quill poised over his ledger. "This is not the best time. Perhaps you can return later —"

"Out!" Nonna said. Renato and Andrea scrambled to do Nonna's bidding. The count remained standing. "You too," she added.

"There can be nothing you would say to Signor Jacopo that you cannot say to me as well. After all, we are as broth-ers." His voice was low and smooth, like a constant murmur.

Madonna! That man knew how to pander. His seamless smile, the ease with which he spoke — I almost half believed him. Then I thought of my rose bushes in thorny heaps and scowled. This man was not my uncle. This man was nothing to us.

"Out!" Nonna commanded again, watching him as he closed the door, then lowering her voice after it clicked shut.

"Have you looked downstairs this morning, Jacopo? The courtyard is a ruin."

"The guards need a place to practice," he said.

"And they couldn't share their space with Flora's roses? Did everything have to be dug up?"

Papa set his quill down and tented his empty hands. "I stand by my decision," he said. "I need an army."

"But why, Jacopo? Our guard has always been sufficient for our needs. What has changed? Are we in danger?"

"This is not the province of women, Mamma. You must leave these decisions to me."

Nonna wagged a finger at him. "Don't you *woman* me, Jacopo. That tone may work on your wife but not on your mamma."

For a moment Papa seemed to return her glare. Then he backed down. *"Bene,"* he said. "There has been a new law passed in the *Signoria*. In the name of public health, Medici troops may now search any shipment of goods and confiscate them as they deem fit. To avoid another plague, he says. Last week in Venice they boarded a vessel of mine that arrived with a shipment from the Orient. Believe me, they were not looking for rats. It's the pearls and silks they're after. I've sent a doctor with two of my fastest couriers to get there and pronounce the ship safe. By the time they arrive, the rats will be the *only* things left."

I suddenly understood why Papa was so distressed recently: the Medici were richer than we were because they were stealing from us.

I looked out the window to the streets of my beautiful city

and the outline of the *duomo*. Today there was no comfort in its splendor. The dome was built with Medici money. Today the walls echoed my father's words: *Medici. Rats.*

Nonna stroked the heavy ring around her finger, as though the black onyx dog were a real pet with soft fur.

"Jacopo, you are trying to marry Domenica to Giuliano de Medici, are you not? What happens if you succeed? Would you wage war on your own daughter, then?"

Papa sighed. "That is Maddelena's scheme. If it works, such an alliance could turn our fortunes. Then I would send Riorio home. All the same, I must take precautions. Certainly you can see that? I do not want to be an assassin for the pope, but I will if I must."

"Assassin?" I hissed. He was not talking about war — he was talking about murder. I didn't understand — the pope was God's chosen on earth. How could my father even think such a thing? "What can the pope have to do with assassination?" I asked aloud.

Nonna explained what my father did not: "While going about God's business the pope entertains lavishly and keeps an army, neither of which is cheap. I would imagine he is heavily in debt to *Il Magnifico*. Am I correct?"

Papa nodded. "He has written that Lorenzo will not listen to reason, and because of this His Holiness would prefer to see a different man leading Florence. One who will not be too greedy to forget the church's share."

"And you are to be the new prince?" Nonna said.

"His Holiness thinks it for the best," Papa said, sitting up straight in his chair as though occupying a throne.

Nonna nodded in understanding. "So he has bid you send for a man who may bloody his hands. That way should Riorio fail, the pope could disclaim the whole endeavor and still look like a saint."

Papa said nothing.

"Isn't that dangerous for you, Papa? I mean, suppose the pope is using Count Riorio because he's expendable. Doesn't that mean you're expendable as well?"

Papa leaned forward in his chair. "That, Flora, is why we cannot fail. We will be joined to the Medici, or we will destroy them and take their place. It is that simple."

I looked out the window. The color of the *duomo* bled into the streets. Everything was now red. And not the orange-red of the rooftops, but a deeper purplish red of human blood. For an instant — just an instant — I knew that if we were lucky, I might trade these walls for those of a convent. If we weren't, if Domenica didn't marry Giuliano de Medici, they would be our tomb.

Nonna got to her feet. "Jacopo, I will speak but once of this matter, then never again. Hear your mamma out: *we have enough money.* The vaults in your bank are full. The galleries in this house are full; your wife's closets are full.

"You say the Medici have taken one shipment in one city. I say to you that there are other, more discreet ports into which you may transport your goods. Therefore, do not be brash. *We do not need more than we already have.*"

Papa looked again at the ledger and shook his head. "Do you not understand, Mamma? This is not about gain. It's about loss."

Nonna grabbed my hand and led me to the door and stopped. "Do as you will," she said. "But there is one thing I insist upon, Jacopo. Riorio may be welcome here, but his men are not. They must find somewhere else to billet. One of them nearly took an ax to your daughter this morning."

For an instant, Papa seemed horrified, and this warmed me. Fatherly concern? Perhaps he thought about me from time to time after all. "Someone took an ax to Domenica?" he said. "Will there be a scar we can't hide?"

I waited for Nonna to whack him, but she did not. Instead, her back grew more hunched as though a heavy load had been heaped upon it. Her piercing eyes developed a dim look. I knew Nonna was old, but she always seemed vital to me — slapping this, swatting that. She may have been old, but she had the energy of ten women. Young ones. Now, for the first time ever, Nonna looked tired.

And what did I do to comfort her? Did I say: never mind, Nonna, it's nothing; I'm used to being treated like this? I'm used to Domenica getting all the attention?

No, I did not. Because the truth was, I was as weary as Nonna. Perhaps wearier, because I never stopped hoping for something different.

Perhaps I *was* a simpleton, because even that day, as we walked downstairs, I waited for my father to send for me. I longed for some service only I could perform. I longed for him to tell me he saw my true worth and that I was too valuable to be sent to a convent.

Emilio was sitting by the hearth in the kitchen, waiting for us. He still had pieces of marble embedded in his head. Nonna bid me attend him while she looked after the patients on the bench outside.

As I picked stone from Emilio's head, I thought that perhaps it was time for me to stop stealing. I remembered how Nonna had looked at my father and said we already had enough, and I took her warning to heart. All this time I thought I was rescuing myself, but instead I was just being greedy like the rest of my family, like the Medici.

It was time for me to be like Andrea and give up the little shards of dreams I hid in my pillow. My family needed me. That had to be enough.

Chapter Six

That evening as I cleared the kitchen dishes, Emilio put up a pallet in the pantry, bonking his head on hanging legs of salty ham in the process. His poor pate was already bandaged so heavily he looked like a sultan.

"What's this? You're setting up camp?" I asked him.

"Nonna's asked me to stay here for a while," he said, re-arranging barrels of red wine and pickled turnips. "I'm going to tend the fire and help you clean up at night."

He was making himself at home, stuffing straw into a mattress with one hand, while eating a full loaf of coarse, round bread with the other. "Why? Don't you have a family of your own?" I asked.

In response, I got a whack on the head. I hadn't even heard Nonna come up behind me. "Don't be rude, Flora. No, he does not. If you'd been paying closer attention you'd know he lost his only sister."

When Nonna said *lost* his sister, I thought she meant mislaid, and that all Emilio had to do was go find her. Then I looked at his face, which seemed to have burned to ash in a matter of moments. I understood what loss really is.

"Mi dispiace," I said. "I'm sorry."

Emilio shrugged, but I could tell more than just his head was smarting.

Nonna spoke to him. "I have had word from Father Alberto. He will meet you tomorrow at the *duomo* after the guard is done practicing." She handed him a purse. "Chances are he won't accept it, but offer it to him anyway. He's a good man."

"Grazie, Nonna," Emilio said, taking the purse. "How can I ever thank you?"

I noticed that he called her Nonna and not Signora Cenesta. He was making himself right at home, this one.

"Just take this one with you," Nonna said, wagging a finger at me. "She needs to get out more."

"Get out where?" I asked. "I get to go somewhere?"

"To Fiesole, Flora. Father Alberto's going to consecrate my sister's grave," Emilio said.

"Why didn't you bury her in a churchyard?"

Nonna answered for him. "Because he had no money."

I looked at Emilio, who nodded reluctantly, the tips of his ears going red.

"No need to blush," I said. "It's not your fault. That's just not fair."

"About time you learned what unfair really means, Flora," Nonna said, handing Emilio a pillow, the coverlet brown with age but still clean. "You think it means your sister gets all the best dresses. You think it means that Renato is your father's lieutenant while Andrea is the one who works. You think it means that your mamma gets to sleep in the finest bed in the house while I content myself with the cell over there."

Nonna pointed to the rickety staircase that led to her tiny bedroom. She was right: it never seemed fair that she should have to sleep above the pantry, her dreams seasoned with the smells of drying sage and leftover turnips.

She was still talking. "We all dine lavishly, *carissima,* even in Lent; we have a roof over our heads. Not everyone lives that way. That is why you will train with our guards. That is why you will go with Emilio and Father Alberto to Fiesole tomorrow night."

"*Aspetta,*" I said. "Did you say I was to train with the guards?"

Nonna rolled her eyes. "What am I going to do with this girl, eh?" she said to Emilio. "We talked about this yesterday when you were mooning about, looking upstairs. From now on, keep your mind on what you're doing. If you had been listening, you would have heard when I said that starting tomorrow Captain Umberto will train you with the rest of his men. He's happy to do it. His conscience is troubling him because of your garden."

"You mean I'll learn how to use a sword?"

"Sword, pike, staff — even ride a horse," Emilio said.

"I already know how to ride a horse," I said, crossing my arms.

"Then he'll teach you not to ride like a sissy, eh?" he said.

If he hadn't been injured I would have thumped him on the head. Instead, I had to settle for stamping on his foot.

"*Basta!*" Nonna commanded. "Yes, Flora, you'll get to learn all those things because you may need the knowledge. Do you understand? The day is coming soon when I won't be able to look out for you."

"That's ridiculous," I said. "We'll be together forever."

"Flora," Nonna said in a strangely soft voice. "I want you to look at my hands."

She held them out in front of her. The joints were so arthritic they bent almost backward. And they shook — her massive ring with the black dog jumped as though it were scratching at fleas.

I hadn't noticed Nonna's tremors before. I looked to her for an explanation, and at the same time saw the clouds fanning out from the center of her brown eyes. She was more than old: she was crippled and blind.

"Listen to me, *carissima*," Nonna said. "Death in one so

old is not a tragedy. I have lived a long life and have few regrets."

"But . . . ," I said, "who will take care of me?"

As soon as I spoke those words I regretted them. For all my thoughts of running away, all my dreams of being free, I was still a selfish little girl, and she knew it.

I looked at the candlelit shadows Nonna and I cast on the wall. I noticed how hers was stooped and crooked, almost as though she had wrapped her frame around a child. Now, as I watched, my shadow grew larger and wrapped itself around her. I would learn to be strong. I would train with the guard and then I would guard her from my true enemy — death.

"I understand, Nonna," I said.

She nodded and withdrew her hands. "I believe you do," she said, fixing me with her hawklike stare.

She mounted the rickety stairs to her bedroom. "And one last thing. You two will not work in the kitchen tomorrow night. You are not to eat with the rest of the guard. Do you understand? When you return from Fiesole there will be a meal waiting for you on the kitchen table. Do not, under any circumstances, eat anything else."

I didn't understand, not about that. Neither did Emilio. But we said nothing.

"Rest easy, Nonna," I said.

"Buona notte," Emilio said.

Chapter Seven

The next day I was in the courtyard before the sun came up, wearing a plain shift, my hair scarved away from my face. I was battle-ready.

The courtyard was completely transformed: there were four targets propped by the street entrance and straw dummies hung from poles on the opposite side. A stockpile of lances and spears and wooden swords leaned against columns, where someone had salvaged jasmine, half-trampled, half-dead. They were for someone else to rescue now. Not me. I had a new job.

I picked up a wooden shield and threaded my arm through the straps. With my other arm I gripped a wooden sword.

Gingerly, I tapped the chest of a hanging straw man. I wanted to see what it felt like and it was *great*. Just for once, not having to behave, not having to be gentle — it was better than cooking. It was better than pruning. And God forgive me saying so: but it was even better than stealing.

The first army to show up that morning was the army of painters led by Signor Botticelli. They came in through the front — five of them, including Signor Botticelli — wielding easels and bags of different things: clear jars, horsehair paintbrushes, brightly colored stones, a rag doll, and sheaths of barley. At the head of them, Signor Botticelli came up to me and kissed my hand that was holding the wooden sword. "Ah! The Flower of Tuscany herself. One day, Flora, I shall persuade your mamma to let me paint you."

"You can stop pandering, Signor Botticelli. I don't have any power."

"My dear Flora," he said. "I am an artist. I must honor beauty where I find it. But, now that I think of it, I have a teeny tiny *piccolo* favor you could grant me. Fill this with a little red wine while your esteemed nonna isn't looking, *per piacere?*"

With a wink, he handed me a wineskin. And Lord forgive me, I took it, even though I knew how Nonna felt about his drinking.

I hid the wineskin in my shift, perching it atop my belt. I don't know why I did. I would never do anything against Nonna's wishes. But for some reason, Signor Botticelli seemed a different sort of man — one to whom rules didn't apply — with his bright velvet cloaks, pretty words, and impish grin that said *there is more to me than you see.*

That was the beginning of my first conspiracy.

At this point, Emilio came out of the kitchen holding a wheel of cheese. "Get away from that one, eh?" he barked at Signor Botticelli. "We need that one. She has work to do."

I wanted to tell him to pipe down, he wasn't my master, but I thought I would let him gain a bit more weight before picking a fight with him.

Instead I looked back to Signor Botticelli. "Do you also need to honor beauty in the boy wielding the smelly cheese?"

The painter smiled, and the smile spread from his mouth to his eyes. "True beauty has nothing to do with what you wield, or even what you wear. Some day I shall prove that to you, Flora Pazzi, Goddess of Spring."

Then he clapped his hands twice and his minions followed him upstairs to the *piano nobile* where the *real* goddess awaited her sitting.

~◎~

That morning we learned how to storm a castle.

Captain Umberto showed us how to advance as one block with our shields above our heads to protect us from flaming arrows. There were no real flaming arrows, yet the task was harder than it seemed. We tripped over each other. When we did, Captain Umberto made us start from the beginning.

"Come on, Giovanni. If this were a real battle you'd be skewered through the eye by now. And the rest of you. Let's move it! I didn't know I was training a bunch of *ladies*."

All the while Domenica's hair flew unfurled like a flag over the second-floor balcony. Her little complaints drifted down to us — complaints about ruining her alabaster skin and sitting still for too long and are you sure holding the barley doesn't make me look coarse? Captain Umberto couldn't seem to keep his mind on what he was doing.

At the end of the day the men packed up to go to their billet, and I plunked my tired body on a bench. I was pleased with what I'd learned today, though I still wasn't sure why I needed to learn it at all. I knew what Nonna told me, and what Papa told me, and it didn't make sense. If Papa lost his bid to replace the Medici we'd just be poorer, wouldn't we? And if Nonna died I would just be shoved off to Our Lady of Fiesole, wouldn't I? I'd grieve for the rest of my life, but I could grieve without shielding my head from flaming arrows.

After a moment I stopped puzzling over it and inspected myself. I was no painting. Bruises were sprouting, more vibrant than *lapis lazuli* but less pleasing to the eye. Goddess of Spring, Flower of Tuscany indeed. No, I knew what I was, and that was definitely not beautiful.

I was also nearly dead from starvation. I wasn't hungry for dainty fare: a pheasant or a raisin, or beans and parsley in thin broth — no, I could eat a whole boar — tongue, eyes, and all.

When Emilio came out of the kitchen, I investigated him for a cheese or a capon or squishy bread, but all I found was Nonna's purse strapped to his belt.

"Where's the food?" I said. "You always have something."

Emilio shook his head. "Remember what Nonna said yesterday? We're not supposed to eat until after we get back from Fiesole."

Madonna! In my training I'd forgotten completely about his dead, unhallowed sister and Nonna's strange request that we not eat until later. What was she thinking, anyway? It was Lent, true, but that never stopped us from imbibing anything.

"Please, Emilio. I'm tired and hungry. Can't I just stay here while you go to Fiesole without me?"

If I were expecting an argument I was disappointed. Emilio just set his lips in a straight line. "Fine," he said, and walked toward the front.

I felt instantly ashamed. Here I was, whining like Domenica after only a few hours without food. Emilio had once gone three days without it. Some soldier I was.

"*Aspetta,* Emilio. Wait!" I grabbed his arm and he swung around, his face filled with righteous fury.

"Are you coming or not? I'm growing tired of your playing. This is just an errand to you, but to me it is my family. My only family. My sister raised me. She was like my mamma and papa and nonna. That's right, my nonna. Think about it, eh? What would happen if that were Nonna lying on unhallowed ground?"

"I would eat later," I said.

"Exactly," Emilio said, and walked away, vindicated.

I followed.

⟡

Once, the previous summer, Andrea and I were in the Piazza della Signoria for a festival. We had been on our way back to the *palazzo* from Papa's bank when our carriage had trouble maneuvering through a crowd. I bid the driver to stop and let us out because I'd caught sight of jugglers in purple and red, and a platform set up in the middle of the square. I was sure we were about to behold a treat.

Andrea had been hesitant but at last done as I wished. "At least pull your veil down before we get out."

I did as I was told and tugged on his hand excitedly. "Let's hurry and get closer," I bade him, pushing my way through the throng.

But he made me hang back, and soon I understood why. As the jugglers practiced off to the side, a girl was led forth in irons. She was young — not much older than I. Her skin was filthy and her hair cropped so close she seemed bald. She was crying and pleading with the two men who held her elbows and dragged her to the platform. She was saying something about not having a husband and children, which I thought odd. If I were a prisoner, I could plead for my children's sake even if I had none.

A narrow man wearing a Medici tunic stood in front of her, faced us, and read a proclamation. I didn't hear the whole thing. I only knew that she had been traveling to San Gimignano and that she had been wearing men's clothing — leggings and a codpiece. She shouted that it was to avoid highwaymen who preyed on innocent women like her, traveling alone without a husband or protector. But the man reading the proclamation didn't seem to hear her, and kept reading to the end.

Something in my stomach sank like a stone. "I changed my mind. I don't want to see this," I said, turning away.

"No, Flora. Now that we're here, don't show them you're afraid. That's what they want."

"Who? That's what who wants?"

"The Medici," he said, gesturing to an upper window in the nearby government palace. A curtain had been drawn back by a jeweled hand of a dark-haired man. I couldn't see him well, but I could see that he was *not* reveling.

Down below on the platform, the narrow man finished reading the indictment and looked up to that same window. I saw the man within nod once, subtly, and down below the man who had read the proclamation took a knife from his belt.

Then the two guards who had been keeping the prisoner on her feet now forced her to her knees. I couldn't see what they were doing to her, but I heard her scream, *no no no,* first in terror, then in a shriek that had no words, just raw pain and horror. The pitch of her voice went up and down like a giant wave. I tried to bring my hands to my ears to block out the noise, but Andrea gripped my fingers tighter.

"*Coraggio,* Flora," he said. "I didn't want you to see this, but now that we're here we have to stay. Whatever you do, don't let anyone see you buckle. You're a Pazzi. We have to stand tall."

The narrow man on the platform stood up and held something small and bloody in his hand that he showed to the crowd. Behind him, the two jailers hoisted the prisoner to her feet, cupping her chin to show her face so that everyone might see. The woman was still shrieking, but her shrieks were now muffled by wet gurgling noises. Deep red blood ran in rivers down the hole where her nose had been just a moment ago.

"Let her try to hide that!" the narrow man said, his fist beating the air in victory.

A cheer arose from the crowd; the woman was dragged off, her nose tossed to dogs as the jugglers took the stage.

I looked up. In a high room in the government palace, a curtain fell back into place.

～⚬～

I thought of that poor woman and her nose that evening as Emilio and I mounted our horses to fetch Father Alberto at the *duomo.* "Eh, Flora?" Emilio said.

"What was that, Emilio?"

"I asked if you needed a veil."

I looked down. My shift was plain, but it was still a dress. And with my long hair I was still clearly a girl. That was the important thing. The authorities just didn't like feeling deceived about a person's sex.

"There's no crime against women going about unveiled," I said. "If there were, every washerwoman in the city would be thrown in irons."

Emilio shrugged. "It's your skin," he said.

My hand involuntarily went to my nose.

∽◦∽

We turned a corner and found ourselves in the shadow of the *duomo*. We trotted the giant length of it until we were in an open space between the cathedral's main entrance and the baptistery building just opposite. The round baptistery was diminutive next to the cathedral and yet, of the two, that was the one that always caught my attention. It was closed this evening, the two doors of the entrance shut tight.

"You fetch Father Alberto," I told Emilio. "I'll stay here with the horses."

As soon as Emilio was out of sight I dismounted and got closer to the baptistery doors, each side containing five bronze panels, each panel molded with different scenes from the Bible. Mamma said an artist named Ghiberti sculpted them. She knew things like that, whereas I only knew the way these doors made me feel. I loved the way the figures were so lifelike, they seemed to jump out at me. I stroked the round curls on the head of Esau in one of the panels and half expected him to turn to me and smile. Surely to be baptized behind these doors meant to be blessed for all eternity.

I tore myself away only when Emilio emerged with my favorite priest.

Father Alberto was a thin man with tonsured black hair clipped above his ears. He wore coarse, gray robes that reached the ground, and sturdy sandals. One simple wooden cross hung from his neck. He was not ornate in his appearance. But his imagination, ah! That was a different matter.

His sermons were more elaborate than Ghiberti's doors. Especially the sermons about hell. He could talk for hours about fiery pits and the writhing torment of the damned. I loved the damned. It was my favorite part of Sunday.

"Flora." He nodded at me. "I haven't seen you at confession lately. Is there anything new you want to tell me?"

"No," I said, mentally going through the list. "It's all the same. I don't honor my mother and father and I loathe my sister. Oh yes, and sometimes I spit into the soup."

"Do you repent any of this?"

"Not really," I said.

He frowned and scratched his head but delivered no sermon, as I knew he wouldn't. Perhaps he thought righteousness was something I could grow into, like Domenica's cast-off gowns.

"All right, then. *Andiamo.*"

ᴥ

The road to the hill town of Fiesole was wide and well-traveled. We rode three across — Emilio and I on horseback, Father Alberto on his donkey. As we progressed steadily upward, I understood the best way to avoid highwaymen is to travel with a threadbare priest. No one looked at us twice. Not even the scrawny ones, their hands twitching around the hilts of their blades.

Emilio told Father Alberto his story, about a different priest who wouldn't bury his sister because there was no money.

Father Alberto sighed. "At least we know he isn't a Franciscan. I hope you do not judge all men of faith by the acts of this one, Emilio," Father Alberto said, wagging his finger. "That priest may be enjoying himself now, but when his day of judgment arrives, he's going to have his entrails pecked out by a giant vulture every day for eternity."

Emilio lit up. "Really? How is that possible? Don't we just have one set of entrails?"

"He'll grow a new one every morning."

Father Alberto then ignited a description that was gruesome even for him, but that I couldn't help noticing sounded like what the Medici did to women who didn't wear dresses.

❧

We reached the town square at sunset and paused to look at the city below. The colors were beautiful: warm reds in a field of green. The River Arno cut through it like gold thread. One by one bright spots appeared as lamps were lit. Soon my father's toadies would start arriving at the *palazzo,* and my family would begin their nightly banquet.

At the thought of food my stomach rumbled. I'd forgotten

my hunger, what with the bronze doors and Father Alberto's talk about eternal torment. "Is it much farther?" I asked.

Emilio indicated a thin path that wound to the summit. We traveled it single file.

At the top we dismounted. A strong breeze blew up here, whipping my hair into my mouth. Unfortunately it didn't taste very good.

Emilio pointed to a dirt mound with a primitive cross, the name *Alessandra* scratched in crudely. It overlooked a valley on the opposite side from the city. It was a lovely valley with sheep and tall grass, dotted with wildflowers. Looking out, I wondered if it were possible for God to dwell in two places: down in my city in the *duomo,* and here among the sheep?

"Emilio," I said. "I don't think you failed your sister at all."

"Really? I could have buried her closer to home, but I always loved this field. I had to carry her body here myself. It was a long walk. There were flies." Emilio stumbled over his words. Nonna was right: he had a heavy load, this one.

Father Alberto removed his wooden cross and kissed it. Emilio and I folded our hands and bent our heads. Father Alberto muttered some words in Latin, but the words themselves were not important.

Standing there at the top of the mountain, with the wind running through my hair, I wondered if Alessandra were here with us now, watching her brother. As I looked at the ground I thought I saw a shadow from the corner of my eye, a restless spirit whipping about our heads, trying to knock us off our feet. I grabbed Emilio's hand and gave it a squeeze.

It's all right, I told his sister. *I'll share Nonna with him. He's a good boy even though he eats a lot. He'll be fine.*

Then Father Alberto sprinkled the holy water, said amen, and we looked up.

The spell was broken. I could no longer weave Alessandra's presence from shadows, or God's presence from wildflowers. The three of us were alone once more.

Emilio dropped my hand and gave Nonna's purse to Father Alberto.

The priest shook his head. "I will not take this. You have suffered enough."

"Please, Father," Emilio said. "Take it. If not for yourself then for the poor."

Father Alberto shook his head. "Don't you see that if I take this from you it will prove a point?"

Emilio shook the purse; the coins jangled. "This is not my money, Father. It is Signora Cenesta's. If I don't give it to you that would be stealing."

"Surely," I piped up, "there is a circle of hell reserved for people who steal from their employers?"

Father Alberto regarded the purse with suspicion, as though if he opened it up a thousand poisonous vipers would pop out and eat his liver every day for the rest of his life. "*Allora.* Here is what we shall do. I will take the purse, but I will not use it. I shall hide it. When you — either of you," he nodded at me, "need money for anything you will come to me. Does that arrangement suit?"

Emilio nodded. "If we do not use it for a while, you can lend it to another worthy soul. Perhaps someone else's sister needs burying."

Father Alberto snorted. "Maybe I could even charge interest. Then I would be a proper usurer."

Then he looked at me and he blushed. He was afraid of giving offense to the daughter of the second most successful usurer in the land.

I took none. Because that day I learned to shield my head from flaming arrows. Even the day before I would not have been offended.

In some ways I had been shielding myself all my life.

Chapter Eight

It was dark when Emilio and I finally returned from Fiesole. The kitchen was empty; and from the pantry came the strong smell of almonds. Nonna must have made tarts for dinner.

The saliva gathered in the corners of my mouth, and Emilio and I raced to the oak table where two meat pies and a flagon of wine were sitting. We finished these, licked our thumbs, and foraged for more. By the time we were done eating, we had consumed three meat pies apiece, one full joint of lamb (bone and all), four loaves of soft white bread topped with olives and seared onions, and one basket of juicy red strawberries.

Everyone was gone for the night, but Domenica and Captain Umberto were sitting in the darkened courtyard, being revolting. We could hear them easily through the open door. He ran his hands through her hair and told her there was never a time he didn't love her.

"And what about the future? Will you always feel the same?" She spoke in a voice just barely above a whisper, but I heard every word: both the ones she spoke and the ones she didn't. My sister was testing him. What she was really asking was: will you follow me to my husband's house and whisper to me in the courtyard when he is away on business?

"Sempre, amore," he whispered. *Always, my love.* Then he kissed her face, with the stinky goat's-milk paste and all.

I heard gagging noises coming from behind me. Emilio crossed his eyes and pretended to choke. "Thank God we'll never be like that," he said, rolling his eyes.

"Grazie a Dio," I agreed. The truth was: I hadn't ever thought about Emilio and me kissing, but that moment when he brought it up I wondered what it would be like. I imagined his breath would smell like old cheese. The salty, stinky kind. Captain Umberto would have the good sense to chew a clove before kissing anyone.

Behind me, Emilio tore into a ham hock. He had the table manners of a mongrel. He was most definitely not my swain.

◦~◦

The next morning Emilio was in the courtyard even before I was, holding a bun in one hand and a wooden sword in the other. He jabbed at a straw man. "Did you hear the news?" he said. "Cesare is dead."

"Cesare?" I tried to remember which one of the guards Cesare was, but I couldn't. I remembered Giovanni and Piero and Ludovico . . .

"You know," Emilio urged. "The one who called you a trollop?"

Then it occurred to me I didn't know which one he was because he wasn't ours.

"You mean Riorio's giant with the ax? The one who pushed me?"

Emilio nodded.

"That was sudden," I said. He had been alive yesterday, glowering in the street along with his *fratelli* opposite the *palazzo.*

"I know."

"What happened? Was there a wench? Did he get in a brawl?"

Emilio shook his head. "No. He died in his bed in a lot of pain. Bit his tongue clear through, he was in such a fit. They're saying it was either poison or the plague."

"The plague?" I covered my mouth and nose with my hand.

"Tranquilla, Flora. No one knows anything for sure. They're billeted with our troops and now they've locked the building. No one may come out. After three days, if everyone else is alive and healthy they will rejoin us."

"*Grazie a Dio* we slept here," I said. "I hate to think what that billet will smell like."

A thought seemed to occur to Emilio and he stopped jabbing at the straw man long enough to express it. "Flora, if everyone else is locked in, who's guarding the *palazzo*?"

My eyes flicked to the street. I was used to seeing three or four men, their spears crossed, sporting the Pazzi *delphine* on their uniforms. And now there was no one between the outside world and us.

"I suppose . . . we are."

We stared at each other with wide eyes, grinning broadly. *Madonna!* This was going to be fun.

❧

The next three days were paradise to me. Not the paradise of my past, alone in my garden, encouraging things to grow — but the paradise of spending time with someone who wanted to be with me. I tried to remember when I had ever had a friend before. The answer was never. Unless you counted Domenica, which I didn't.

During the day, Emilio and I clambered to and from the roof, being lookout. Emilio said he saw pirates. I said: who needed pirates when we had foot traffic? Below us, people quarreled and haggled and drank and exchanged gossip. Once, a drunken harlot in the building across the way exposed her buttocks to the window and pooped on the street below.

I thought this was highly entertaining. The poor soul passing underneath her did not.

We capered with our wooden swords and laughed so hard, Mamma looked up to the roof and turned away, and Domenica looked up from where she was posing for Signor Botticelli and shook her head in disdain.

Signor Botticelli was the worst. He would paint a couple of strokes, then look at us, then look back down at his subject. We were making it hard for him to focus on his work. After two days of this he threw a jar of blue paint from the balcony.

"Bah! I cannot concentrate with this racket!" He grabbed something from his backpack and strode up the roof toward us. Emilio and I sat in a corner and tried to look as though we were well-behaved.

When he was at the top of the ladder, Signor Botticelli called me over. "You two!" he said loudly. "Do you want me to have you thrown off the roof? Fie on you! I can't work like this!"

He pulled a jug from his cloak and handed it to me. "Here, hide this up here," he whispered. Then he scurried back down the ladder, all the while swearing about what troublemakers we were.

Once he was gone, I showed Emilio the jug. We hid it in the eaves under a loose tile. "That is one strange man," Emilio said.

"He's an artist. Artists are like that."

Emilio shrugged and the two of us went back to playing lookout.

There was an easiness between the two of us that I had

only felt before with Nonna. Perhaps even more so, because one day as we sat there watching the foot traffic below, I even told Emilio of my plan to get to Venice. I told him about the fourteen flawed diamonds sewn into my pillow.

"I thought about giving them back after Riorio came," I said. "Andrea says we need every florin. But now I don't know. I know what Papa would say, and I know what Father Alberto would say, but I also know what I feel."

"And how is that?" Emilio asked, sipping from a skin of water (he said we shouldn't eat while we were on duty).

I thought hard. "Cheated," I said.

Then Emilio, my new and only friend, laughed at me. He laughed so hard I thought his brains would spew out through his nose.

"*Cretino!*" I said. "Who do you think you are, making fun of my misfortune?"

"Come, Flora. You must admit this is funny. What can you possibly feel cheated out of?"

"A life of my own?" I said. "A husband? A man who isn't a wastrel like you?"

Emilio wiped tears of laughter from his cheeks and his mood settled. "I can see you are sorely abused, you who have a nonna who loves you and looks after you. Sometimes, Flora, I forget that you are like Domenica."

"I am not!" I said, poking him in the chest with a wooden sword. "You take that back!"

Emilio just pushed the sword point away. "You may not

want to hear this, but it's the truth. Look around you, Flora." He pointed to the Bargello prison, but three houses away from us down the Via dei Balastrieri.

"For the past hour some poor soul has been screaming nonstop. His cries curdle my blood, but you don't hear them. Look below, at all the activity going on. These people are scrambling for their daily bread. To you it's just entertainment. Very few in this life get what they want, Flora. The rest are used to it. Why not you? Why do you keep asking for perfection? I think you are very spoiled indeed."

I thought of the prisoners' screams and the beggars scrambling to earn their bread, not to mention the endless line of patients benched outside the kitchen, waiting for Nonna. How could I tell him I was used to them? The suffering of others was part of the landscape. It didn't affect me. Not here, safely inside this guarded castle, doubly cocooned by strong walls and my capable nonna.

He was right: I was spoiled. But I didn't tell him that. "I ask for perfection because I am not a coward," I said instead. "Is it not bravery that urges me to pursue a better life?"

Emilio shook his head. "You dream big, I grant you that. But dreams are funny things. I always dreamed of being a soldier."

"Bene," I said. "You should understand then. You *are* a soldier. You changed your life. You could have stayed in the country, but you didn't."

"I couldn't have stayed, Flora. There wasn't enough food,"

he said. He looked out over the rooftops to the hills of Fiesole. "You're right, I did change my life. Being here? Of use to a lord? This is all I ever wanted. I should be happy, but when I'm at my happiest I'm also at my worst."

I didn't understand. "Why is that?"

He looked at me as though I were simple. "Because I never would have had this were my sister alive. Don't get me wrong — I loved her dearly. But had she lived I would still be working the fields. If I had taken a wife, I would have had to work harder still to feed my family. And no matter how hard I worked, there would always be some winter like this last one when there was not enough food.

"Instead my belly is full and I play on a rooftop with the daughter of a wealthy man. No, Flora. For Alessandra's sake, I must never forget that my happiness is built on a grave."

This seemed dire even for him. I had no quip ready on my tongue. We were no longer playing.

Finally, Emilio looked up and spoke. "You would never make it to Venice. You wouldn't even get as far as Bologna," he said. "There are men on the roads waiting for girls just like you. Girls who have spent their lives in *palazzos* and carry Papa's diamonds."

I understood the thrust of Emilio's words. I would not be able to present my real face while on the road. I would have to be someone else. "Then I won't travel as a girl," I said.

His eyes popped and then narrowed. "You would get caught."

I examined myself. I could almost pass for a youth now, with my arms and face red from the sun, the dirt under my fingernails. Perhaps I wouldn't be like that other girl, the one in the *piazza* separated from her nose. "Maybe I wouldn't. Look at me, Emilio. I'm already half man."

Emilio's eyes traveled up and down, taking me all in. When he was done, he shook his head. "You're not half man," he said. Then repeated: "You would get caught."

Another scream ripped the air, coming from the Bargello. This one I heard. Someone must have abused the Medici terribly to deserve such a fate. Or perhaps not. Perhaps it was just someone like Emilio who had to do something drastic to eat. Whoever he was, I said a silent prayer that he was not in too much pain to dream.

"Those poor souls," Emilio said, crossing himself. "Signor Valentini will be laughing for sure."

"Signor Valentini doesn't exist," I said. "He's just a tale made up to scare children who don't eat their supper."

Emilio just shrugged. "Alessandra used to tell me that there was a real Signor Valentini who lived in the Bargello and that he was the cause of all the suffering in the world. But maybe you are right. Maybe he's just something people made up to scare children into behaving."

He jumped to his feet. "*Allora,* it's getting late. We should help Nonna," he said. He started away but then turned back. "Keep your diamonds for now. Your plan is flawed, but perhaps there is another way."

I shut my eyes tight against the screams. The lights in back of my closed lids looked like a million cramped white stitches in a bed of lace. Then I opened my eyes and stood up to join him.

This is what I knew: I did not want to go to a convent, thank you very much, a threat Mamma made yearly but thus far I'd escaped. I'd been to My Lady of Fiesole: it was dark and cramped inside and the sisters smelled like overcooked fruit and went blind embroidering undergarments.

I also knew that I liked my nose where it was — not in the gullet of some mongrel. I sincerely hoped Emilio was right, and that there was another way. Maybe if I served my family well enough they would see my true worth. Maybe I would be allowed to stay. Not marry — that was too much to hope for. But maybe I could take over Nonna's place and be a cook and a healer. That might not be so bad. Especially if I could reclaim my garden. Nonna's existence was hard work, but at least she had a measure of freedom.

Chapter Nine

That night, when the guests had departed and the stacks of dirty plates were mountainous, Nonna told us the story of my namesake.

She was standing by the kitchen hearth, whacking burnt logs into embers, when Emilio asked if Flora were a family name.

"No more than Lorenza, which is the name her mother gave her. I was the one who called her Flora, because for as long as she has lived, she always preferred to be outside. But I'm not sure I did the right thing. The legend of the goddess Flora — it's not a pretty story."

I wondered: how could a story about the Goddess of Flowers not be pretty?

Meanwhile Nonna, satisfied with the state of the fire, sat heavily on a chair by the oak table and peeled herself an orange.

"Go on, Nonna," Emilio said.

"Like my granddaughter here, Flora is not the original name of the Goddess of Spring. Flora is just her Roman name. In Greece, before she was Flora, she was a human child named Chloris."

I plunged dishes into dirty water, trying not to act too interested. Chloris. An ordinary name. I liked it. In my household the stories were usually about other types of girls — the pretty ones. They met good ends or bad, depending on how meek they were. Only rarely was someone like me the hero.

"Chloris's mother, Niobe, was the Queen of Thebes," Nonna went on. "She was a proud, vain woman with seven daughters and seven sons. She was so puffed up with importance she bragged about her fine children to the gods, who were dreadfully angered. Especially Leto, who had but two children, Apollo and Diana."

I searched my memory. Apollo, God of the Sun, and his twin sister Diana, Goddess of the Moon and the Hunt. Not meek, those two. Especially Diana. She liked to turn people into stags and set her vicious hounds on them. Nonna was right: this story was not going to be pretty.

By now there was one long thin spiral of orange peel on the table. Nonna planted her thumbs in the middle of the fruit and broke it into sections. Instantly, the air around us tasted sweet and tart.

"Fourteen children," Nonna said, shaking her head. "Slaughtered before their mother's eyes. But I find it hard to pity Niobe. She was a silly woman, more concerned with her station in life than her real flesh-and-blood family."

"So how does Chloris come into this?" Emilio asked as he scraped tiny bones from dirty plates into a bucket.

"Chloris was the youngest. She asked Diana to spare her just before Diana let her last arrow fly."

"It must've worked, if she went on to become a goddess," Emilio said.

Nonna shrugged. "Her end is different depending on who you ask. Some say she was killed along with the rest. But most believe that Diana took pity on her and spared her life, then banished her from sight, doomed to wander the earth forever, chased by Zephyrus, God of the West Wind."

I thought of Fiesole and how the wind made me eat my own hair. I could easily believe in a gale strong enough to keep someone running for years. I pitied Chloris in her plight: confused, exhausted, just wanting to sit down, but every time a moment of stillness comes over her the wind whips her to her feet and the chase begins anew.

"What changed?" I asked. "What turned her into Flora?"

Nonna leaned back in her wooden chair, savoring this detail as if it were the freshest honey. "There can be only two answers. The first is that the gods finally took pity on her and turned her into a deity. Or else she herself finally developed the courage to stop running and confront her fate."

Nonna finished the last section of her orange. Emilio stood wiping the same plate he'd wiped when the story began. "She must have been very brave to stand up to a god," Emilio said absently.

"Exactly," Nonna nodded, wagging an orange peel at us. "That girl had *coraggio*. But a different kind of courage from those other heroes. The rest of them sought their glory, always rowing off to this island to kill the minotaur, that one to capture a golden fleece. They rained their heroism down on them. But Flora? She invited nothing. All she did was stand tall in her tragedy. That takes real strength of will."

Nonna looked me in the eye, sending some message I didn't quite understand. But I think it was this: *I know what you suffer. I know about your diamonds. Stay put. Stand tall. You will emerge divine.*

Nonna sighed and tossed her orange peel into the fire. "I am weary. Be a good boy and help me up the stairs," she said to Emilio, who was already at her elbow.

With the two of them gone, I attacked the rest of the dishes, trying to bring the mountains of dirty plates down to hillocks. I plunged a pile into a basin of water and had soap up to my elbows when I heard someone cough.

I turned around. Signor Botticelli was sitting on the

bottom step holding an empty goblet studded with rubies. Sweat was pouring from his forehead, and he mopped it up with a pristine white handkerchief.

"What are you doing here?" I asked.

"Getting away from your dinner guests. I needed to breathe," he said. "That Riorio likes to make speeches. Long ones. Tonight I thought about braiding my own nostril hairs to quell the boredom. Which reminds me: where's the wine? That should help my disposition."

I nodded toward the pantry. "Help yourself," I said, and went back to the dishes, hoping that now that he had what he wanted he would be on his way.

Instead he came back and placed two full goblets on the table. One for him, and another for me, presumably. He then picked up a clean rag, and without another word, wetted it and ran it over my face.

"Hey!" I said, and swatted at him as though he were an angry bee.

It didn't seem to bother him. When he was done he merely pinched my chin with his hand and turned my head to the right and left. He seemed to be looking for flaws. I'm sure he found plenty.

At last he let me go. Party sounds wafted downstairs. "There's beauty enough in the great hall. Why do you have to pick on me?" I asked.

He wrinkled his nose in disgust. "Above stairs? There is an abundance of beauty. Beautiful gowns, beautiful music, beautiful table settings." He examined the jeweled goblet. "But none of it really nourishes."

"*Bene,* as long as you're here, make yourself useful," I said, and handed him a clean plate. Then another. He dried each and made no sign of leaving.

"I think your nonna must be the most beautiful woman in the world," he said.

I put down the dish I had been cleaning. I had never heard her described this way. Even those grateful to her for healing and feeding them often called her a witch. But I thought of the crooked shadow she cast, and suddenly the air was suffused with sweetness, as though someone had just torn into the flesh of an orange.

"I think so too. Her care — it cripples her, but it also makes her beautiful."

Signor Botticelli nodded in agreement. "I wish I were painting her instead of your sister."

I stared at him.

"Close your mouth, Flora. It is unbecoming," Botticelli said, taking a long drink of his wine. "Your sister is lovely, but for art something more is needed, *which* I finally found. It wasn't an easy task. Everyone should start calling me *maestro.*"

With that, he drained his goblet and reached for mine. I let him have it. His face was growing florid with drink.

Maestro indeed. Whenever I walked past him and my sister the easel was always covered. To my eyes all he did was arrange hair and bunches of grapes, then later drink *our* wine from *our* goblets and call *our* guests boring.

"What did you do?" I asked. "Wipe her face?"

"No, no," he said, sitting down and propping his dirty boots on the oak table. He was apparently done drying dishes. He unbuckled his girdle and hissed out a very strong but contented sigh. "It was something she did. It happened the other morning when the sun was shining and you and the guard were practicing in the courtyard. I had her seated with a doll on her lap meant to represent the baby Jesus. I was thinking of painting her as the Madonna enthroned. But then someone cried out from below and she turned her head."

"Probably Giuseppe," I said, remembering. "I trod on his foot."

"Don't interrupt," he said. "*Allora,* I saw her stare at the captain of your guard with a look so full of longing and sadness. . . . It was that touch of sadness that made her beautiful. Your sister may lead a charmed life now, but she will not be charmed forever, and she knows it."

I stared at him again but was careful to keep my mouth closed this time. Domenica? My Domenica sad about anything? The one beautiful enough to have both a lover and a husband? The one blessed with parental approval?

Perhaps there was something in his words. Of late her smile had grown more forced and she spoke faster when she wanted something. Perhaps Signor Botticelli was right, that this was the happiest Domenica would ever be, and, conscious of this, she had quickened with anxiety.

Emilio came out of the pantry, his eyes shooting arrows at our guest. "What are you doing here, eh?"

"I came in search of more little barrels," Botticelli said, raising his goblet in a mock salute. "How do you think I got my nickname?"

Emilio's eyes went to our guest's ungirdled stomach, which was substantial. His eyes darted to me. Botticelli. Little Barrel. Why would a person choose to call himself that? Either it was because of his build — a little barrel of a man — or he drank a lot of little barrels of wine. Emilio now was in the unpleasant position of calling Signor Botticelli fat or calling him a drunkard.

"More wine, Signor Botticelli?" I asked, reaching for his empty goblet.

"Signorina Flora, you are a goddess among women," he answered with a wink.

I took a candle with me and went into the pantry. In the dim light I kept bonking my head on haunches and sprigs of things that were strung from the ceiling. At last I stumbled into the wine barrel and dipped the goblet in it. When I came out my head was covered in slivers of prosciutto and dried rosemary.

Standing in the dark on the threshold, I caught a flake of conversation between Emilio and the artist.

"Why does she labor down here? Why is she not above

stairs with her sister, wearing pearls and playing the mando-
lin?" Signor Botticelli was asking. "She is a Pazzi just as much
as the other."

I shrank back into the darkness, taut with fear. It was as
though someone were about to shoot an arrow at me. *No. Not
this. Don't tell him this. It's not a pretty story.*

". . . like an unwanted batch of kittens. Can you imagine?"
Emilio was saying.

"These noblemen are not like you and me," Signor Botticelli
replied. "What a brood. Still, I like to think if you or I already
had eleven children we would love the twelfth just as much."

Emilio replied: "Signora Cenesta tried to tell Signora
Maddelena that Flora's head was normal, that babies who had
spent a long time in the birth canal often looked like that and
that hers would be less egg-shaped with time.

"But Signora Maddelena still could not be persuaded to
nurse Flora or even look at her. They say that Signora Cenesta
had to pull Flora out of Signora Maddelena with a tool they
use to shoe horses. Perhaps when she looked at Flora she saw
her own pain."

"You're conjecturing now," Signor Botticelli said, wagging a finger. "But perhaps you are close to the truth. You're
probably too young to remember, but twenty years ago
Signora Cenesta was formidable. She dined above stairs every
night and men came from far and wide to listen to her counsel. And now what's left of her? A shabby old woman who
makes poultices and stirs the soup."

"Mind your tongue, *signore,*" Emilio said. "She's been kind to me."

"She's been kind to the whole city," Botticelli said. "Yet the fact remains that she is a shadow of what she once was."

"What are you suggesting?"

"I'm saying that perhaps Signora Maddelena only *threatened* to drown Flora like a sack of kittens because she saw that someone wanted her more than she did."

"You think that Signora Cenesta gave up her position as head of the house in exchange for raising Flora."

There was silence for a few minutes; the clatter of plates being stacked in a cupboard.

"Flora says she was supposed to go into the convent, but she's fourteen years old and still here. You think that is Signora Cenesta's doing?" Emilio said.

"At one time that woman had the ear of kings," Botticelli said. "Keeping Flora by her side would be nothing for someone as cunning as she."

I didn't like hearing Nonna called cunning, but then again, I didn't like to hear any of it. I'd heard the story dozens of times before. The message was always the same: I was an ugly baby and would bring my family no fortune through marriage. I was no use to anyone.

Now I heard Emilio sigh softly. "What a family, eh? A bunch of *cretini.*"

"No, Emilio. It will not do. You cannot keep Flora and

Signora Cenesta and cut out the others because they are un-pleasant. They are part of the tableau as well."

I'd heard enough. I came out of the pantry and shoved Signor Botticelli's goblet at him. It slopped over onto the table and his pristine linen tunic.

With a glare at Emilio, I lifted my skirts and tromped up the back stairs, the soft wood worn into troughs by years of my heavy footfalls carrying things to and from the kitchen.

As I walked I felt split in two. The firelight and Emilio's plain speech combined with his soft voice made my tragedy seem like just another story — one that happened to someone else, someone who grew up and was turned into a laurel bush or who fired golden apples into the sun.

But there was another part of me that couldn't stop shaking. I'd heard the story dozens of times before, but it always ended with Mamma not wanting me. ("And why should she?" Domenica would end. "She already had *me*.") Until tonight I'd never heard the part about Mamma using me to bargain her way into mistress of the house. Was it a lie? I didn't think so. This much I knew: that when my *nonno* first died, Mamma should have taken over her position as mistress of the house immediately. But she didn't. Instead the house was ruled by Nonna, who, like Lucrezia de Medici, had grown too formidable. Something then must have happened to make Mamma and Nonna trade places. I never thought it was me. I always thought it was business transacted outside my realm.

And yet Emilio was right. There was much truth in Mamma's neglect. As Signor Botticelli said, it was a conjecture, but a good one.

Before tonight I'd been torn about the nature of the tragedy of my life. I could never decide if it were because I wasn't beautiful, or because as a plain girl, I could never bring my family fortune.

But now I understood my real tragedy, which was that Nonna loved me too much.

True, without her I might have ended up in the bottom of the Arno. But then again, maybe not. Without Nonna, Mamma might have accepted me eventually. I might never have had to become Flora. I might have remained Lorenza Pazzi, noblewoman, garlanded with parental approval, soft and luxurious as the finest velvet brocade. I would have walked through the house like Domenica, my tread so light it wore down nothing.

But it was not to be. Instead I was forced to look for other ways to be of service to my family. As I fell asleep — the outline of my diamonds pressing themselves against my cheek — I didn't yet know how I would get away. I only knew that Nonna was wrong: standing tall was not enough. If I stayed here I would never turn divine. I had to be more like the other heroes — the Greek ones — who sought their monsters. I had grown weary of the ones in my own home.

Chapter Ten

The next morning I accosted Andrea on his way to the library. He was walking down the Madonna gallery with his nose in a book. How could he walk and read at the same time? I feared he would trip over that bust of Dante.

"*Fratello mio,*" I greeted him.

He looked up and smiled indulgently. "Flora," he said. "When are you coming to the bank? We've had a new shipment of tapestries and table settings to inventory."

Tapestries and table settings. Some debauched prince had defaulted on his loan.

"Whenever you need me," I said. "But listen, I have a question for you."

From the great hall came sounds of Signor Botticelli arranging Domenica and ordering around his minions. I drew my brother out to the balcony and lowered my voice.

"What would be the best way to get to Venice?"

"You're not planning on going, are you, Flora?" he asked with a laugh. "You would get robbed and left for dead before you got to Fiesole."

I tried to laugh myself but could not. "No, not me. I was thinking of someone more like Emilio."

Andrea's face took a serious turn. "*He's* not planning on leaving, surely? He's so trustworthy. We need more like him."

"Not that I know of. Come now, Andrea, surely you can see I'm just curious. What would it take? How much money?"

Andrea seemed to relax. I was engaging in an intellectual enterprise, spinning thoughts from thin air. His second favorite thing in the world after dropping things from great heights. "Not money, Flora. In fact you'd have to guard your money well. If I were a youth traveling alone I would ride hard and keep to the main roads and pray no one knew I possessed any wealth. And even then I would carry a weapon and not be afraid to use it. No road on the peninsula is safe."

I patted his knee. "*Grazie,* Andrea. Since I cannot leave this place I must travel as I can."

I stood up to go back in.

"Flora," Andrea called to me, his face suddenly wrinkled with worry. "Are you sure you want to know how one person could travel? Not two?"

I knew what Andrea was asking. He wanted to know if Emilio and I were planning on running off together. "I am sure, Andrea. I have no plans to leave. With or without Emilio."

"It's just that . . ." He stood up now. The door behind me back into the gallery was half open. He closed it with a soft click. "I am not blind, Flora. I know you could never be happy as a nun. I also know that, for whatever reason, our mamma has no plans to find you a husband." He leaned in close. "If you really needed to know how two people could slip off to Venice, I might be able to help you. But not now."

"When, then?"

"Ideally? Never. I would miss you too much. But there is a strong wind blowing from the south. One that may change our fortunes."

I was surprised. In Florence, winds most often blew from the north. But Rome was to the south. Andrea was talking about the pope.

"Easter is next week," he continued. "Our mother has it in her mind to have a great feast the night before and has invited the Medici. She hopes to unveil Signor Botticelli's masterpiece at that time."

"A feast? The night before Easter? That woman is crazy."

Andrea just shrugged. "If it works, there may be no need for you to leave. Else there may be every need. I tell you, I do not care for Riorio's counsel. He is too *practiced* for my taste."

"I promise you, I shall take no action before Easter."

"Bene," Andrea said, and I moved to open the door.

He closed it again. There was some problem bothering him more than usual, one he turned over and over in his mouth like a grain of sand. "There is one more thing. Heed carefully what Captain Umberto has to teach you. We should all be preparing as you are."

Andrea's hand was still on the door, keeping it shut. He needed some reassurance from me. A reassurance I had yet to give him.

"Fratello mio, you worry for nothing. I swear to you we will grow old together, dropping weights from the roof just to see how fast they fall."

He released the door and opened it a crack, only mildly satisfied. "That is my fondest wish, Flora. All the same, I fear our fortunes are what are falling. Fast."

⁂

I left Andrea and went downstairs to find Emilio. He was standing in the entranceway to the *palazzo* under the dolphin coat of arms in a formal pose. His had his formal tunic on, his *mazzochio* firmly in place. I couldn't help but notice that he had changed since he first came here. Today he only looked slightly ridiculous as a guard. At least his cap stayed on straight.

"What are you doing here? I thought we'd play lookout."

"Nonna just got word. Captain Umberto and the others

return today. No one has sickened since the death of Cesare, so the doors to their billet were unlocked and our men are able to come and go as they see fit."

"*Bene,*" I said. "Then I will stand with you."

Emilio and I stationed ourselves in front of the *palazzo,* our spears crossed, the way we'd seen the others do. People on the street nodded as they walked past. "*Ciao,* Flora! *Ciao,* Emilio! Lovely weather we're having."

"Stop smiling and waving," Emilio groused. "We're supposed to look imposing."

I did my best, but the idea of being imposing sent me into a burst of the giggles. As far as I was concerned, standing around with a spear was no different than looking out for pirates. Then Nonna came out with two raisin puddings for us, and I stopped doing even that.

"How goes the watch this morning, *ragazzi?*" she asked. She too thought we were playing.

Emilio threw up his hands. "This one will never be a soldier," he said, pointing to me.

"Even soldiers have to eat," Nonna said, and poured him a mug of water.

It was at that moment, with our guard relaxed, that the men came back. There were seventeen in all: twelve of ours, five of Riorio's.

I hoped our troops hadn't grown too chummy with Count Riorio's men. I still hated them for destroying my garden (even though one of them conveniently obliged me by dying for it).

But when they came sauntering down the street, I realized that whatever had happened as they were locked in, it was not what I imagined.

To begin with, they held themselves apart from one another. Riorio's men walked on the opposite side of the street. Captain Umberto and the rest were careful to keep themselves between Riorio's men and the *palazzo* at all times. The mood was strained; Riorio's men spat and muttered the whole way.

All seventeen were pale and emitted an unholy scent. Three days with no way to empty chamber pots? No wonder.

Then I noticed that one of ours, Piero, was even paler than the rest. When he drew near I saw him stumble. Captain Umberto offered him an arm, and as he did, I noticed there was a filthy, bloody bandage wrapping his left hand.

Madonna. What happened to this poor soul?

Nonna acted quickly. She unwrapped the bandage. His hand was caked with blood. I stood with her and poured water from my mug over the blood to see the extent of the wound. It looked as though someone had speared him through the palm. "Take that one to the kitchen," she said to Giovanni. "Tell Graziella to give him all the wine he can drink. The next hour will not be fun, but he'll live."

Despite the warning, Piero seemed relieved to be under Nonna's capable care. "*Grazie,* Signora Cenesta," he said, as the two scurried past.

Riorio's men huddled to the right of the entrance. The

worst one, the one who dug at his nose with his blade, took out his dagger now and threw it at an imaginary target in the ground.

At that moment I realized that while I didn't know all that had passed in the billet these three days, I knew enough.

Nonna took a good whiff of the air. It was *foul*. The stench clung to the men's hair and clothes.

She threw a purse to Captain Umberto and told him to get his men to a bathhouse. "And don't just rinse your faces and necks. Get your whole selves into the water. I'll send Graziella with clean linen."

Nonna sniffed the head of Riorio's goon. A fly buzzed out of a lock of his hair. "It couldn't hurt you to go with them," Nonna said.

His only response was to toss the knife and pick it up. She grabbed him by the earlobe. "I'm talking to you, simpleton."

I think I knew what was in the air even before Nonna did. This is what I knew: Nonna couldn't help being Nonna; the one with the flies around his head was too quick with his blade.

The man jerked Nonna's hand off his ear, slammed her against a wall, and put the knife to her throat. "Keep quiet, old woman. We don't answer to you."

As soon as he was on his feet I threw myself on his back, scratching at his face, trying to gouge his eyes. "Get away from her!"

I was little more than a nuisance, but it seemed to work.

The man took his blade away from Nonna's neck and sliced my forearm. The pain was fierce but I hung on tight. Emilio yelled a deep and terrible yell and twisted the blade away from him. I thought he would wrench the man's arm right out of its socket, he was so rough.

The goon changed his tactic and slammed my back against the wall. Still I hung on, furious. Nobody treated Nonna like that. I brought my good arm up to his greasy head and yanked out a handful of hair. He roared terribly and slammed me again, this time jerking me free. Then he pitched me into the street as though I were a sack of straw. I landed in the muck.

For a moment my head swirled so badly all I could see was spires. When I looked up at least ten daggers were out of their sheaves (ours) and pressed against human flesh (theirs). Real daggers — not wooden ones, of which my bloody arm was evidence.

Captain Umberto sat on the chest of the man who started it all, pointing a knife at his throat. "Enough! I don't care who your master is," he said, with a look so ferocious I thought he must no longer be a man, but some beast intent upon the kill.

He had his blade close enough to the man's neck to draw a drop of blood. He didn't relax his grip. I crouched there for a moment, then two, then three. Then, when I thought it was over, Captain Umberto gave an inhuman bark, brought the knife up to the man's face, and made a deep, jagged cut along his cheek.

I found myself backing away, looking around for Emilio only to find him suddenly cushioning my back, cradling my injured arm. I shook despite the warmth of the spring air. *"Tranquilla,"* he whispered. "Be calm." But his voice was tense.

I reminded myself to breathe. Of all the things that had happened in the past few minutes — the knife drawn on Nonna, the breaking of my own skin — what scared me most was the look on Captain Umberto's face as he cut that man.

Riorio's goon brought his hand up to his cheek but didn't make a sound. The look on his face was terrible — full of hatred and darkness.

Captain Umberto stared back at him with a look just as dark. "I've divested you of your good looks. Threaten any of the women of the house again and I shall divest you of something else."

He stood up, walked over to me, and offered me a hand. *"Va bene,* Flora?" he asked.

"Sì," I said slowly, standing up to my full height. I was terrified of him in this moment, but in one part of my mind, the one beyond fear, I knew Umberto was being so terrible because of us. I knew who the real enemy was, and I was not willing to let them see me cower. "It's just a scratch," I said as he examined my arm. Indeed, it was. A long cut but not deep.

Emilio stood next to me, watching Riorio's men retreat across the street. He drew in saliva as though he were going to spit, but Umberto put a hand over my friend's mouth. "No," he said quietly.

I looked around. Nonna was back to her normal stooped posture, twisting her black-dog ring around and around her finger. Piero, the only other one bloodied, was already in the kitchen getting drunk enough that Nonna could sew him together. All that lingered was the unholy scent, which I no longer minded.

But there had been damage done there that day. I looked again at the blood on my arm and felt as though I had just been baptized.

Captain Umberto bowed to Nonna. "A word with you please, *signora,*" he said.

Nonna nodded and the four of us — Emilio, Umberto, Nonna, and I — went inside the courtyard.

We left behind us ten of our men, each one standing tall. As they crossed their spears, it didn't look as though they were playing at all.

When we were out of sight of the street, Captain Umberto leaned forward into a marble column, breathing heavily, as though he were about to vomit. I understood what this episode cost him. This is what it took to keep my sister's skin fair and her neck decorated with pearls.

"You were right," Umberto said to Nonna. "Three days locked in with those rats was enough to make animals of all of us."

"Did you discover anything?" Nonna asked.

"Not a thing," Umberto said. "Other than they are not to be acted on like regular men. This proves it," he said, pointing to my arm.

I nodded as though I understood what they were talking about; but I understood nothing. What had they hoped to discover?

"It is worse than I feared," Nonna agreed. "I'll prevail on my son yet again. Perhaps it's not too late for him to see reason. For all our sakes, I hope this party Saturday is a success and we can call Domenica Signora de Medici."

Captain Umberto's head snapped up at the mention of her name. "Saturday?" he said. "So soon?"

Nonna nodded. "I know it pains you, but it's for the best."

"It's all right, Signora Cenesta," he said wearily. "This winter I would never have wished such a thing. But after today . . . 'twould be enough were she safe."

Umberto clenched his eyes shut then stood upright. When he opened his eyes, he was once again a hero — the one with the easy smile and the soft words. Not the dark menace of a man who had slashed someone's face only a moment before.

He came over to me and ran a hand gently through my hair. I felt the motion in the tips of my toes. *Say it,* I thought. *Call me* amore *just once.*

"You," he said. "You two have not been idle in our absence." His look went from me to Emilio and back again.

I felt pain in more than my arm. His words were kindly meant, but they were not what I wanted to hear.

"Yes," Emilio said with sarcasm in his voice. "We were very effective against men of straw."

Captain Umberto nodded once. "You did well against men of flesh too," he said. "But you're right to be afraid. If the feast is Saturday we don't have much time." He took his hand off my shoulder. "Get cleaned up," he said to me; "this afternoon we'll teach you to use a staff. I think it's a better weapon for you against a larger foe."

Chapter Eleven

Nonna directed a bath for me to be poured in a tub in her room. I kept a damp cloth on my arm and immersed myself in the warm water, grateful for the time to be away from the rest of the house. I liked Nonna's room. It was quiet and spare — there was just a cot, a trunk, a cross over her bed, and a bronze relief of a dog against a wall. It hung just about waist high. If I were standing I would have to bend down to see it, but since I was in the tub I could regard it easily.

I kept thinking about what had just transpired. Nonna and Captain Umberto's words in the courtyard kept echoing in my head. *You were right. They are animals.*

The two of them had spoken so easily, almost as though they were teammates.

Not teammates, I realized, conspirators.

But conspirators in what? *Billetted for three days together. Discovered nothing more.*

But the men were only locked in a house together because it was thought Cesare died of the plague. No one could plan that, could they? How do you manufacture an act of God?

I heard muffled voices coming from the corner of Nonna's room. I shrank down in the tub. "Graziella?" I called timidly. But she wasn't here; there were no footsteps on the creaky stairs. I was alone. What was that sound?

I looked around: the voices seemed to be coming from the bronze dog. I knew I'd seen that dog before but couldn't remember where. Finally I realized: it was the same dog as on Nonna's ring.

There it was again: a low voice — no, two low voices.

I grabbed a linen towel from where it was lying on a trunk and wrapped it around myself. I went up to the wall with the dog and put my ear to the wood paneling. What *was* on the other side? I had thought Nonna's room bordered only the pantry.

I put my hand out to stroke the head of the bronze dog, and a wall opened on silent hinges. I sprung back.

Inside was a dark, cramped space filled with stoppered vials. I smiled. Nonna had a secret room. I was glad. She had too little around here.

I grew bold and took a step inside. The ceiling was low and I banged my head on a beam. I crouched down. The room was so dark, I had to feel in order to see. I knocked something over.

"What was that?" a voice said, a male voice. It was coming from the other side of Nonna's stoppered closet. I stood still and held my breath.

"It was nothing," said the second voice, my father's. "That fireplace creaks from time to time."

Carefully, I picked up what I knocked over — a glass vial with a symbol of the black dog etched on it. I also noticed one ceramic goblet — not the good kind, like the ones used in the great hall, but the ordinary kind, like the ones we used to serve the guards their meals. I brought the goblet to my nose.

It reeked of almonds.

I turned in the direction of the voices and pressed gingerly on the wall. It was heavy, but it swung open slightly. My face grew hot as though it were on fire. And then I realized where I was — behind the hearth in Papa's library.

"You have stalled too long, Jacopo." This was the second voice, the one I recognized as Count Riorio's. "You are no innocent, remember? You've promised the pope he would be rid of the Medici this week. His Holiness will not be pleased if you waver."

"I am not wavering, Riorio. Believe me. I just need time."

"Time for what? We are not weak men. We must act."

"And we shall. After tomorrow night's party."

I heard something slam, like a ledger on a table. "Tomorrow night and tomorrow night. I'm telling you, my men are back. The time to strike is now."

"Prudence, my dear count. *Il Magnifico* and his mother and brother are coming to the feast in person. I want to see how they function together. Lorenzo is growing bolder in the *Signoria,* but I suspect he is not the one we really need to worry about."

"You think Giuliano is more formidable?" Riorio said.

"No. I'm talking about their mother, Lucrezia." Papa chuckled. "I know from experience never to underestimate old ladies."

I heard a sigh, then Riorio spoke again. "I see. You are unwilling to act because you are worried about retribution from someone's mamma."

My father said nothing. Count Riorio continued, his voice polished slick: "There are those who say you are not really with us. They say that you are secretly plotting an alliance with the Medici."

"Why would I do that, Riorio? I hate the Medici as much as you."

"Why do you do anything, Jacopo? For profit, of course."

In the silence that followed, I thought it must be clear that Papa was lying. "*Bene,* after tomorrow night then," Riorio said. "Delayed action for the prudent man it shall be.

"While you are being prudent, Jacopo, keep this in mind: today is Friday. Sunday the pope's army arrives at Porta Romana.

They expect to support the new ruler of Florence. That man can either be you, or it can be someone else. Someone who knows how to treat old ladies."

I remembered Nonna earlier today with a knife to her throat, and I realized that Nonna and Captain Umberto had been conspiring to rid us of Riorio's army of rats.

I had heard enough. I closed the door as softly as I could and backed out of the closet.

There, holding my clean shift, stood Nonna.

Chapter Twelve

P ut that down," Nonna said, her skin as gray as her hair.

I had forgotten I was holding a goblet. "Put it down!" she said with more force.

I set it back on a bench in the dark room. I'd never seen Nonna this angry. She was a tiny woman, but in her wrath she was a giant.

"Did that thing come anywhere near your mouth?"

I made no reply. I was still as a bronze statue.

"You heard, girl. Did you put your lips on that goblet? Did you take a drink?"

"It was empty," I finally blurted.

She examined me as she would one of her patients, lifting my lids, opening my mouth, glancing under my arms. What was she looking for? *"Bene,"* she said finally, yanking me out of the dark room and slamming the door shut behind us. Then she plunged my arms up to the shoulders in the tub and scrubbed them until my wound reopened. I bit my lip to keep from yelping.

When she was done, she toweled me off and handed me my shift. "Put this on and sit over there." She pointed to her narrow cot. I did as she said.

She paced the room, shaking from head to toe.

Watching her pace, I began to suspect something, although I didn't dare give it a voice. I'd once heard that arsenic, when heavily used, smelled like almonds. Perhaps that was how someone could manufacture an act of God.

Finally, Nonna plunked herself down on the other side of the bed and sighed. "This could have been much worse," she said at last.

"Please, Nonna. I didn't mean anything. I just heard voices. I wanted to find out where they came from."

"I'm not mad at you, Flora," she said, placing her gnarled, spotted hand over mine. "I'm just a scared old woman."

"Shall I get you some wine, Nonna?"

"No, *cara mia*. I am fine. But when I saw you standing there holding that goblet, I thought the time had come for me to pay for my sins."

"What sins? What aren't you telling me?"

Nonna stood up. "I am not ready to disclose all, *cara mia,* much as I love you. But I think I may share part of the story."

She pressed the bronze dog again. The door sprung open. "This passage was built by your ancestor, the original Pazzi — the knight your father keeps bragging about. The knight used it. His son used it. All the Pazzi men have used it, even your grandfather, my husband. Each and every one an adulterer. They would select their kitchen maids based on their looks and then house them here in this room. Then they would use that passage to slip away from their wives and come down here. Your nonno swore he wasn't like the rest. He was a sinner, but he swore he would stop. He never did. So I made him stop."

I looked at the black-dog ring on her finger. She was spinning it round and round again, the way she always seemed to do when she was vexed.

Poison. I said the word to myself. Nonna was not only a healer, she was a killer. She was telling me as much: she had killed my grandfather.

Was I shocked? Perhaps. But not as much as I should have been. She was still Nonna, stooped and gray and beautiful.

"I had hoped your father might be different. But now I know he's like the rest. He merely traded lechery for greed and moved his deviousness to the *Signoria.*"

"Papa? Devious in the *Signoria*? I thought he worked in the open."

Nonna shook her head and closed the closet door. "Haven't you learned by now? No one in this town works in the open. Not even me."

❧

That night I had trouble getting to sleep. When I closed my eyes, expecting to call up brisk winds and azure seas, instead I just saw a large, black dog. The more I tried to make him go away, the closer he came. It seemed to me I could smell his fetid breath and see the flies buzzing around his head. His teeth were sharp as daggers.

With this image in my head, it was no wonder that I was still awake when Domenica came in for the night. She carried a lone candle that cast an eerie glow all about us. She rustled out of her skirts and into her nightdress, muttering all the while. *"Stupida, stupida, stupida."*

Then my charming, beautiful sister let fly a word that would have made even Count Riorio blush.

"Domenica?" I said.

There was stillness on the other side of the room. She blew out the candle and crawled into bed.

"Domenica?" I tried again. "Are you awake?"

"No," she said, flipping over.

"Is something wrong?" I asked. I didn't really think she'd reply other than with a complaint or a command. Maybe, if she were in good humor, she might say *get me some cheese* or *fetch another candle*.

Instead she did something completely different. "I feel

like a chicken!" she said, and burst into the most ferocious bout of crying I had ever heard.

"What are you talking about?" I asked.

Her crying slowed. "I've been *plucked,*" she said. "Mamma said she had to do it tonight so no red spots would show on my face tomorrow."

"And that's a problem?" I asked. "You pluck all the time."

"I pluck the hair on my head and sometimes those little downy ones on the lip. But this was different. I begged her to stop, Flora! But she wouldn't listen. She told me to shut up, that I would bring shame on the House of Pazzi."

I listened to her snuffle a little more, still not understanding. So Mamma had overdone it with Domenica's hair. Was that really worth crying over?

Domenica spoke again: "It's funny how a person can take little things for granted. Like eyebrows."

"She plucked off your eyebrows?"

"She said all the fashionable women were doing it and I should keep still about it. But I don't like it at all. It makes me look *ugly.*"

That sent her off into a fresh round of tears.

It was dark so I couldn't see her face. I tried to imagine what she looked like.

"Is Mamma sure it's fashionable? The Medici won't think you look like a ghost?"

"She said she'd paint thinner, more delicate eyebrows with tar."

Tar and goat paste — all that on a person's face. And to what purpose? Domenica's natural eyebrows were perfectly fine. "That doesn't make any sense," I said. "Taking something off to put it on again."

"Easy for you to say." She was growing surly now. "Mamma never pays any attention to *you*."

I frowned. "Excellent point, Domenica," I said.

At least the crying from the other side of the room had stopped. Not slowed — stopped entirely. It was as though she had blown out her feelings the way she'd blown out her candle. "That woman keeps finding flaws," she said, talking more to herself now than to me. "Nothing is ever good enough. If I stay there'll be nothing left of me. She'll pluck me into oblivion."

With her words I thought I began to understand a little of my sister. Perhaps we were not so uncommon, she and I. She wanted to stay here, in the garden. But the garden was gone, and like me, her path wasn't clear. Others were constantly telling her what her path *should* be. Perhaps, for all her bluster about having both a husband and a lover, she was scared.

"Domenica," I said. "Take it from someone who's been around a lot of raw chickens. You look nothing like that. You will never look anything like that. No matter what Mamma does to you, she cannot make you less beautiful. You have something underneath the face paint and gowns. Signor Botticelli sees it, I see it, Captain Umberto sees it. Why can't you?"

In the silence that followed, I realized I'd gone too far in mentioning Captain Umberto's name. It was as though I had opened a wound.

Domenica just sighed. "I've got a long day tomorrow."

And that was all. She didn't say she'd try to get some sleep; I knew she couldn't. She didn't call me sister; I knew somehow she couldn't do that either. All we exchanged were a few whispered words in the dark.

That night, no matter how much I smoothed down my pillow, the lumps of my fourteen diamonds conspired to bite me in the cheek.

Tomorrow would be a long day for both of us.

Chapter Thirteen

When I woke the next morning Domenica was already awake. Not only awake — awake and humming.

She threw open the shutters and twirled in the morning sun. I saw what Mamma had wrought yesterday. Yes, her eyebrows were indeed gone. Not only that, Mamma had plucked the hairs off her forehead so high she looked like half an egg.

Whatever had happened to her yesterday seemed to make no difference to her disposition today. "Come on, lazy," she said. "Get up and get me some strawberries."

I threw off the bedcovers and reached for my shift. I wasn't upset Domenica had become herself again. I needed to get to the kitchen anyway. There was much work to be done. Fifty live eels were to be delivered this morning, along with cages and cages of squawking pheasants, barrels of olive oil, and pounds of goose liver for a thick sauce. I thought we should just slaughter a pig and be done with it, but Nonna said the Medici prefer lighter, squirmier fare. Guess who got to hack the heads off our dinner?

I walked out the door and down the hall, my thin slippers making no noise on the wooden floor.

"Where do you think you're going?" Mamma stood in the hallway, clapping her hands to get my attention. She was uncoiffed, her dark hair falling around her waist.

"To the kitchen?" I said. It was more a question than an answer.

"Nonsense," Mamma said, taking me by the arm. "You're a part of this family and it's time you start behaving that way instead of scurrying below like a rat. Now get back in your room and wait for the ladies' maids. I'll have your grandmother bring you and your sister up a tray with something to eat. But don't eat too much. You need to fit into a tight gown tonight."

She noticed the bandage on my arm. "You'll need long sleeves," she said.

This was the first I'd heard about dining in the great hall with the others. I thought I was going to serve. I wasn't pleased. Neither, apparently, was Mamma.

I plunked myself back on my bed in our room. "Couldn't you just tell the guests I'm a kitchen wench?"

"I thought of that," Mamma said. "But your father already told *Il Magnifico* that we have two unmarried daughters. I don't know what possessed him."

I caught myself thinking: *for profit, why else?* He probably wanted to trot me out this once and see how much money he could get if he married me off. I was a resource, a flawed diamond.

Domenica and I spent the whole day seated in our room in front of the glass. Four maids bustled between us while Mamma hovered behind and barked suggestions. "A little more under the eyes." One maid brushed my hair off my face and was about to start plucking when Mamma stopped her. "Don't spend too much time on this one," she said, looking over my shoulder. "All she has to do is curtsy and she's done. Right, Flora? You won't actually say anything tonight, will you?"

"Not if I don't have to." As far as I was concerned, I was going to say as little as possible and then skulk in some corner, a fake smile masking my face.

At the end of a long afternoon, one of the maids trussed me into a simple gown (*simple* meaning there are only four rubies on the sleeves instead of a whole vault) and Mamma shooed me down to greet our guests, although how she expected me to do this without talking, I didn't know. Domenica was still in her shift, humming a tune and admiring her reflection when I left.

I didn't bother to look at my reflection. I was ill-suited for dresses and I knew it. If Emilio saw me he would probably laugh and call me a sissy.

It was early evening when I stood on the threshold to the great hall, admiring Mamma's handiwork. The place was certainly festive tonight — lovely with the soft light of the lamps all around, the rich brocades of the ladies, and lively music from minstrels. Most of the guests had already arrived. I saw Renato and his wife, then my eldest sister Beatrice and her toad-faced husband, Paolo, all the way from Naples. Over by the balcony, Andrea was engaged in earnest conversation with a philosopher from Pisa.

Il Magnifico himself was wedged in a corner. He was a dark man with a brooding face and lean build. His tunic was wine red; his leggings were black. He was talking to another man — one of Papa's colleagues from the *Signoria*. He pressed his forehead against the other man and whispered to him and patted him on the cheek. I imagined he used words like *love* and *ally*, but the word he was thinking was *control*.

"So, we're not good enough for you anymore, eh?"

I turned around to see Graziella, the kitchen maid, red-faced from either drink or strain, holding trays of cooked eel in sage and oil. *Madonna!* Did this woman have to make every exchange an insult? She was wearing a new velvet tunic over her dress. The symbol of the Medici *palle* was on the front; the *delphine* from our coat of arms was on the back. Mamma must have had them made special for tonight. She was sparing no expense. If Mamma would have listened to me, I would have told her that it seemed too presumptuous, that wearing the Medici coat of arms does not make us Medici.

"You might be interested to know that since *your ladyship* deserted us there is twice as much work for the rest of us," Graziella said.

I frowned at her. "Mamma's not ready for the main course to be served yet."

She slapped the dishes down on a stand in the hallway. The eels jumped from the plates as though they were alive. She stood back and put her hands on her hips. "I hope your guests like their food cold, then. Because I'm not taking that back to the kitchen for warming. It's too heavy. Your nonna expects too much from me."

I shrugged. Suit yourself. It didn't bother me if the eels went cold. It wasn't my party.

I thought she'd go back to the kitchen, but Graziella came and stood next to me. I didn't like being shoulder to shoulder with this woman. I didn't even like being in the same room with her. She was lazy. I wished she would leave.

But she didn't. She wasn't done taunting me. "Lovely night," she said. "Everyone in Florence must be here. But I can tell you who isn't here. Father Alberto."

I forced myself to breathe. Not Father Alberto. I liked Father Alberto. A fact she knew and was using to her advantage. The best I could hope was that she would be done insulting me quickly.

"He stopped by the kitchen earlier. Said it wasn't becoming for clergy to attend such a feast the night before Easter. He said Christ is still dead and He doesn't rise until tomorrow and that the town should still be in mourning until then. He said Satan would roast him like a pig on a spit if he crossed your threshold tonight."

I was afraid I would redden with shame. I didn't know if Father Alberto had really said that, but he would have been right. I thought back to the first day Emilio came to the *palazzo,* and how the two of us had been listening through a half-open door when Mamma compared Domenica with the Queen of Heaven. Even then she had been setting us too high. And tonight, looking at the spectacle and the two coats of arms on the servants' tunics, it felt to me as though our fortunes were a tender babe she'd carried to the top of the leaning tower and was holding over the railing. All I could do was watch it drop.

I told Graziella none of this. "Twice as much of no work is still no work," I said, drawing myself up. "I suggest you get back to the kitchen before Nonna finds out and allows you to *not work* in the streets."

Graziella walked away muttering. "You just wait, Flora. God will strike you all down."

Fine, I thought. Let her mumble; let her threaten. She was not clergy. She had no right to speak for God.

I looked back to the great hall. I thought to myself: one unpleasant encounter over with. Surely the rest of the evening couldn't be much worse?

Then I heard a swish of skirts, and my sister came to join me.

She stood next to me on the threshold while four maids fussed with her skirts. Now properly done up, she looked luminous. Her eyebrows had been expertly painted; she wore a delicate gold headband that looked like a halo; her dress was pale pink — almost white. There were gems sewn into the sleeves of her gown, little lights winking here and there from her wrist to her shoulder. On closer look those gems seemed puny for the lavish effect she was trying to create. I even spotted a flaw in one. A very familiar-looking, rabbit-shaped flaw.

She stood by me and her smile became a smirk.

Suddenly, I understood.

She had cloaked herself in my future.

I felt the heat rise to my face. I was so furious I shook from head to toe. I wanted to throw her over the balcony and have her land in the muck. I wanted to smear her face down in horse poop until the fake eyebrows came off and then parade her in front of the guests. See? Under all that goop she's just half a rotten egg.

But I thought of Nonna and Captain Umberto and held back. Good people, not Domenica, wanted this marriage. I resolved to keep calm. Tonight I would behave like a daughter of the House of Pazzi. As soon as the party was over I would go straight up to her room and throw her brush in the chamber pot.

"Let me attend my sister," I said to the maids, my smile growing more practiced by the moment.

When they were gone I pretended to busy myself with a loose thread on Domenica's train.

"Why?" I whispered through clenched teeth. "Why did you need *these* stones?"

"You should thank me," she said. "I won't tell anyone you've been stealing."

"You have no idea what you've done."

"Lower your voice, sister," she said, hiding her mouth behind a sachet. "I have every idea."

Domenica fluttered her eyelashes and looked demure. I felt as though I would explode like cannon fire in a moment. And yet I kept pretend-plucking at the back of her dress, hoping to find the one thread that would unravel her completely.

"I am fifteen years old, sister," she continued. "I should have been married at twelve. I've heard noblemen whisper at dinner. They say I must have something wrong with me that holds suitors back. One even said that I've had congress with the devil, and under my skirts I have the legs of a goat."

I produced a laugh that wasn't so forced. Half devil indeed.

"Mamma has worked on me day and night, picking me into nothingness. And what have you done? You've been running around free. You came and went as you pleased. You called me names behind my back. Don't think I haven't heard.

If I had had just one kind word from you or Nonna in all this time . . ."

For an instant I looked up, and her face was not a mask. Then it was again. "Besides," she whispered. "What need do you have of pretty things? They would only make you seem plainer than you already are."

Mamma approached; her hair also woven into plaits; her gown the color of rich red wine. "Ah, here they are," she said. "My two blessings." She held her hands out as though to embrace the two of us, but kissed the air around Domenica's head and not Domenica herself. Me she left alone.

She locked her arm in Domenica's and turned her back to me. Just as well. Tonight I didn't mind being discarded. Mamma steered Domenica to a fine lady with white skin and a straight nose (no lower-class ridges like on Mamma's). Her gown was woven throughout with gold thread.

This must have been Lucrezia de Medici, mother to Lorenzo and Giuliano.

Signor Botticelli bustled about Signora de Medici, fetching her more wine, more mushroom tarts. "Toady," I muttered under my breath. Signor Botticelli had spent every evening with us for the past week in the kitchen. I'd grown fond of him. He was a strange man, arranging even broken dishes so they made a pleasant scene. Tonight I was beginning to see that it didn't matter. Up here he was the same as all the rest.

Domenica stood in front of Signora de Medici, her hands

clasped chastely in front, her eyes on the floor. Even while I hated her I knew she was beautiful.

Signora de Medici didn't agree. "She is a fine girl, of course," I heard her say, "though I fancy not so fine as my own Bianca. Her posture is fair, her hair is tolerable. . . ."

Pick pick pick. Domenica was right. She was being plucked into nothing. That didn't excuse her, but it helped me understand her a little.

And then, like Signor Botticelli, I grew dizzy from an overabundance of beauty. It seemed to me everyone's smile was too tight, everyone's gown too elaborate. I made my way to the balcony, closing the door behind me.

I leaned over the rail. *Tranquilla,* I urged myself as I gasped.

"Are you all right, *signorina?*" a man said.

I wheeled around. There stood a young man in a fine black velvet doublet and cape, carrying a goblet. I only saw half his features in the lamplight, but they seemed more polished than handsome. His chin was smooth; his hands uncalloused. A heavily jeweled cross hung from his neck.

I didn't know who this man was, but he was clearly a nobleman. I had to behave.

I curtsied. "I'm fine, thank you. It's just a bit crowded in there."

I looked at the marble-tile floor and clasped my hands in front of me the way I'd seen Domenica do.

"You're not . . . are you Domenica?"

"No," I said. "I'm her younger sister, Flora." I should have given him my real name, Lorenza. But I was unused to pandering.

"Flora?" the man asked. "The one they treat like a servant?"

I looked up and stared him in the face. "How did you know?" I blurted.

The man shrugged. "My brother has spies all over the city. He probably even knows what you ate for breakfast."

"Your brother," I repeated. "Are you Giuliano?"

He nodded once, then leaned on the railing. He handed me his goblet of wine. I drank deeply before handing it back. Behind us came the sounds of forced laughter. Neither of us made a move to go back inside. We stood together, watching the festive lamplight below. Someone had made the fountain work again, and it made a pleasant gurgling sound.

"You don't seem disappointed that I'm not someone else," Giuliano said.

"Neither do you," I replied.

"My brother is the darling of the family. I've never been as quick or intelligent as he. Mamma calls me a wastrel."

"My mamma calls me a rat. She says I'm always scurrying."

It was a quiet moment. I wished I could spend the evening out here forever, not talking, not saying the wrong thing, not being inspected, and most of all not thinking about what I was going to do tomorrow.

Then I ruined it. "Are you going to marry my sister?"

Giuliano didn't look at me. He didn't seem offended, but

neither did he seem surprised. It was as though he had been expecting me to ask. "Your sister is indeed beautiful. But not as beautiful as my . . . ," he trailed off.

"As your what?"

"That's the problem. I don't know what to call her. I would like to say my wife but she is not. Nor can she ever be. Carolina, the woman I love, is not one of us, as my mother daily reminds me. She is the daughter of the man who manufactures cannons. He has a shop on the other side of the Arno by Fort Belvedere. She tends his customers. I think her the most beautiful woman in the world."

"Ah," I said. I understood this was the moment my family feared. Giuliano was trying to tell me politely there would be no marriage.

I shivered a little in the night air. It was only April still.

"Mamma says I don't love Carolina," Giuliano continued. "She says I'm just dallying with her and that's to be expected. But I know what I feel."

"Your mamma can't know everything," I said. "Has she ever been in love?"

Giuliano pursed his lips. "I doubt it. Her marriage was a political alliance."

I nudged his arm and pointed to the revelers inside. Their smiles looked like frescoes — something plastered on. "Look at this crowd. Does anyone look like they've ever loved someone else? Or are they just amusing themselves? If you ask me, they're the wastrels."

This thought seemed to amuse him. "I am indeed grieved to cause your sister disappointment," he said. "At one time she was a true candidate for my wife. But it wouldn't have been the same, you know. She would have had my money but not my heart. Then my mother decided she wasn't good enough and that was that."

"Thanks," I said mildly.

"Come, Flora, don't be that way," he said, giving my arm a friendly shove. "I wasn't insulting you, I was insulting her — my mamma. *Nobody's* good enough for her. Other than Christ, that is. Mamma has bought me a bishopric. She says the family needs someone to look after both the goat and the cabbages. Meaning our fortune and our status with the Lord, I suppose. Someday she hopes I'll be the first Medici pope."

"Will you be?"

"Probably," he said. "Pope Sixtus is heavily in debt to my family. It seems these days even the highest of holy offices can be bought."

I tried to act surprised.

He looked back over the courtyard and drained his goblet.

"Did I tell you I have a son?" he said. His tone was that of an old friend trying to catch me up on the latest news. *Have I forgotten to mention what we ate last Tuesday? Have I forgotten to mention I fathered a child?*

"No."

"It's true. He's still a babe, but I think my boy the most

handsome Medici ever. Nothing gives me greater joy than spending an hour with him in our garden, just watching him smile and coo and pass gas. It grieves me he will never carry my name."

I turned my head away. I didn't want to hear any more revelations. I didn't want to like him. But it was already too late.

"Perhaps it's for the best," I said, not looking him in the eye.

"What do you mean?" he said.

"Maybe if he doesn't have your name he won't have your responsibilities. Maybe he'll be free to make his own choices."

Giuliano regarded me openly. "Freedom, eh?" he said. "What a lovely thought."

I could only silently agree.

Then his face clouded over and he took my hand in his. "Flora, I have enjoyed talking with you. Promise me you won't think ill of me."

I thought of my family's fortunes, which hinged on this man's fancy. I thought of the words my mother used: *Secure his alliance. Secure his regard.* And I realized that of all the silly, devious things my family has plotted, trying to gain security through love was the most foolish.

"I promise," I said. "When are you leaving for your bishopric?"

"I go directly after high mass tomorrow," he said. "Why?"

So you will be in a sanctuary when Riorio puts his plot into motion.

"You'll take a guard with you, naturally?" I said.

"I usually do."

"I was just worried about highwaymen," I muttered. "One of our couriers nearly got his throat cut on the road to Fiesole the other night."

He patted my hand congenially. "You're a kind girl, Flora," he said. "I know what it is to be cast in shadow by an older sibling. But I've also learned that just because my brother is fiendishly clever, that doesn't mean I'm a dolt. Do you understand?"

I nodded, but I didn't. Not really.

Seeing my confusion, he pressed on. "I just wanted to tell you that even though everyone thinks your sister the beautiful one, that doesn't mean you're ugly. There can be two beauties in your family just as there can be more than one man of business in mine."

He turned to go.

"Hold fast to what you love, Flora. Don't let anyone take it away from you. And don't — and I mean don't — let anyone sell you into the church."

He was joking. He was talking about himself. He knew nothing about my future at Our Lady of Fiesole, I was *almost* certain. All I could do was chuckle along with him. Then he bowed and kissed my hand with ease, a nobleman with natural grace. And I saw how manners, when properly used, didn't need to be weapons. Sometimes they just put you at ease.

When Giuliano opened the door to rejoin the party, my mother was standing there, staring right through me. The expression on her face was cold as marble.

Chapter Fourteen

Inside, the guests were already seated and munching contentedly. The plates of eels had already been cleared away and everyone was addressing their roasted pheasant with plums and goose gravy. Mamma pointed a bony finger to an open seat on the far end of the dais, away from the people who mattered. In the center, *Il Magnifico* was talking to Papa, covering Papa's hand with his own.

I found myself seated next to the head of the goldsmith's guild, a man named Girolamo, who was apparently Signor Botticelli's old master. *Poverino.* Signor Botticelli never stopped talking about how much he hated being apprenticed to the goldsmith, how he never felt he served his artistic vision in that smelly furnace. And yet this man seemed congenial. Most of him was red as though he'd been excessively scrubbed for the occasion, but his hands were black with soot. He regaled me with an appraisal of every necklace in the room, putting my own paltry countinghouse talents to shame.

Count Riorio was seated even farther away from the center of things than I. He spoke to no one as he spooned soup to his mouth. His eyes darted around the room.

And then the moment I dreaded arrived. A covered easel was brought in, and Signor Botticelli stood in front of us, resplendent in a velvet cloak lined with ermine. He did not smile, but his eyes twinkled with delight. This was his moment, and he was pleased.

My father called the guests to silence and made a pretty speech. "We have had the honor of a master artist in our midst these past weeks. He has deigned to use my daughter Domenica as a model for his latest Madonna. We are humbled and pleased to present this painting to our city's other great patron of the arts, Lucrezia de Medici."

Signor Botticelli stepped forward. He held himself erect, his piercing eyes meeting those of everyone seated on the dais. He also wore a smug smile, as though he were better than anyone else in the room and he knew it. He still spoke with distinction. "Signor Pazzi, Signora Pazzi," he nodded. "I thank you for your hospitality. Your daughter is the loveliest young woman I have ever known. If I have captured only a fraction of her beauty, I will have done my work."

A dainty pheasant bone stuck in my throat.

He clapped his hands twice, and the two assistants threw the cover off the easel.

I dropped my knife and gaped openly.

For there, for all of us to admire, was a Madonna lovelier than any painting I have ever seen. It even put Ghiberti's gates of paradise to shame.

There were three figures in the painting: the Madonna herself, a Christ child on her lap, and a curly-haired angel standing next to them. The virgin's face was that of Domenica but the expression — ah! I remembered Signor Botticelli telling me that she was only beautiful when she was sad. And this was a very sad Madonna.

Next to the Madonna, the angel offered her a plate of grapes and wheat. The same kind of grapes and wheat we used to make bread and wine. The same kind that must have been used to make Christ's last meal.

Surely, I thought, this has to be a symbol of the Eucharist.

The Madonna reached out to accept the wheat. I realized: that's what makes her so sad. She knows her child, this jolly baby on her lap, will have a last supper. She knows he's going to die.

I looked to Giuliano de Medici, father of a young son

himself. His face registered shock, and I knew that I was right.

Next to me, Maestro Orazio whispered. "Sandro was right to change careers. That's as fine a painting as any I've ever seen. Look at the pathos."

Lucrezia de Medici stood up and inspected the canvas, a fake smile playing about her lips. "Signor Botticelli, you have outdone yourself. Look at the fine brushstrokes and the rich colors. Signor Pazzi, I accept your fine gift. I thank you and compliment you on your choice of artist and the beauty of your lovely daughter . . ."

Mamma beamed. This was the moment she had been waiting for.

". . . who someday will make some lucky man a fine partner."

"Some man?" my mother said. The turn of her face was terrible. How she could scowl and still be smiling, I didn't know.

"Indeed," Signora de Medici said. "It is a pity we could not secure her for Giuliano, but my younger son has just announced his intention to go into the church. He will take high mass tomorrow in the *duomo,* then after that he leaves immediately for Siena. It is my fondest wish that upon his return he will be celebrating mass as well as receiving it."

Around us there was polite applause. Giuliano nodded in embarrassment.

And Mamma? No amount of goat's-milk paste could hide

what she was feeling. "I see," she said, keeping her voice steady as she stood up. "Pray excuse me. I must see to something in the kitchen."

With that, dinner was over. The rest of the guests stood up and pushed themselves closer to Signor Botticelli's master-piece.

I was not able to see the canvas close up, and knew that when the last guest left tonight my opportunity would vanish forever. This art would not be hung in our gallery; it would not be hung in the *piazza*. It belonged to the Medici.

Signor Botticelli stood apart, playing the part of successful artist. But at least some piece of him must belong to us, his comrades below stairs. It was that piece that I wanted to speak to. I pushed my way up to him and kissed him on the cheek. "Thank you," I whispered in his ear, then I ran away. I wanted him to know that at least one of us truly saw and appreciated his work.

As I ran off, I thought I heard him call in a voice that wasn't practiced. "Flora, wait, please . . ."

But I had no more time to spare for him. Thanks to Signor Botticelli's painting I knew what I had to do.

The sad eyes of the virgin. The features were Domenica's, but the expression was Nonna's. At last I understood. All Nonna's grisly warnings, the half secrets, the whacks upside the head. She behaved like a woman who knows her child is doomed. But she was not like Signor Botticelli's Madonna, blandly accepting the grapes and the wheat. She was a fighter, that one. And she was fighting for me — for all of us.

There was a war coming all right, but it wasn't going to start in the *Signoria*. It was going to start in the kitchen. Mamma needed someone to blame for tonight's catastrophe, and I knew exactly who it was going to be.

I heard Mamma's voice before I set foot over the kitchen threshold. She no longer wore good manners like delicate jewelry. She shouted and gestured, her hair loose from its plaits and her face looking like an avalanche — the white paste on her face melting off in globs.

"I have had enough of you," she yelled at Nonna, who sat quietly peeling an orange. "For years I've tolerated your presence. Changing orders. Undermining my rightful spot as mistress of this house. What did you think: that you could marry your own son?"

Emilio stood behind Nonna like a guard.

"From now on I give the orders," Mamma said. "Do you understand? I plan the menus; I deal with the riffraff outside; I decide who goes where."

"What do you mean riffraff?" I said. I brought myself between Mamma and Nonna.

"Quiet, Flora," Nonna hissed.

"You," Mamma said, looking right at me, her eyes narrow with hatred. And in that look I understood that I had been wrong about everything. I had been wrong to assume that if I worked hard enough she could be persuaded to love me. I had been wrong to think that, had Nonna not taken my part when I was an ugly babe, Mamma would have accepted me. Without Nonna I would have met my fate at the bottom of the Arno. Mamma would not have loved me if I looked more like Domenica; she would not have loved me if I added to the family fortune; she would not have loved me if I were a nun; she would not have loved me if I made a brilliant marriage.

Even knowing this, all I could do was place myself between Mamma, whom I didn't like, and Nonna, whom I loved ferociously.

"The one night I expect you to behave and what do you do?" Mamma said. "You turn poor hapless Giuliano into a complete bumpkin. Tell me: what potion did you slip into his wine, you *strega*?"

I balled my hands into fists at my sides. I looked her in the eye and didn't blink.

"She's not the *strega*," Emilio said, lurching forward. Nonna pushed him back.

"So now the kitchen boy is giving orders?" Mamma said. "Don't tell me this isn't your fault as well, old woman. Surely you can see why I won't allow this state of affairs to continue."

Then Mamma turned her attention to me. "My beloved Lorenza. Last child and comfort of my old age," she said sarcastically. "It is clear to me I should have taken a firmer hand with you. As it stands, I see the work of the devil stamped on your flesh."

"That's enough, Maddelena," Nonna said, her voice even.

"I don't think you understand, old woman. *You* don't get to say what's enough around here anymore. It's my turn. And now I'm telling you: *enough*. I'd kick you out if I could, but your son would never allow it." She leaned in and stared Nonna in the face. "But you will be punished.

"Flora," Mamma said, without taking her eyes off Nonna. "Pack your things. Tomorrow you go straight away to Our Lady of Fiesole. I shall instruct the sisters to keep you in a dark cell and deal with you severely until the devil loosens his hold on you."

She smoothed her hair, and with a whisk of her skirts left our realm.

For a moment all we could do was stare. Then Emilio broke the silence by hurling a dish at the spot where my mother just stood. It shattered to the floor.

"*Bestia,*" he said.

He sat down at the table by Nonna and buried his head in his hands.

"*Tranquillo,* Emilio. She hasn't had the last word. Nonna's got something planned. Haven't you, Nonna?"

I looked at her and flicked my eyes toward her room, hoping she'd take my meaning. At that moment I could have administered poison with my own hands.

Nonna did not seem to feel the same way. She shook her

head. "No, Flora. We will not plan anything. Don't you understand? She's your mother. We can't act upon her the way we act upon others."

"There's got to be something," Emilio said. "Please, Nonna. I'm not worried about you. One month with the household under that woman's care and you'll be back in charge. But this is the wrong thing for Flora and you know it."

Nonna looked up at him and shook her head. "Maddelena has made up her mind, son," she said. "And tonight I haven't the teeth for vengeance. You two shouldn't, either."

I didn't feel the same way. I had teeth enough for all of us. I wanted to tear into her raw flesh, carve the anger and entitlement right out of her face.

"Allora," Emilio said. "We have to do something."

"And what would you do? Would you have Flora stay here? Even if she stays it won't be as it was before. No, Emilio. Don't you understand? If you two do anything tonight you may win and get your way, but staying will turn Flora into one of *them*."

That shut us both up.

"Look at her, Emilio. Look at her face. She is not the same girl she was this morning. It has already begun."

No, I thought. I'm not like them. I'll never be like them. But I remembered the way I'd ordered Graziella back into the kitchen and I knew Nonna was right. It was time for me to leave. But to the convent? Was I really going to allow myself to be locked away? I didn't see what else I could do. As Emilio said: freedom demands money. As of tonight I had none.

"There comes a time when we all must grow up, Flora," Nonna said. "Your time is now. We will not fight. We will pack. We will sleep. And tomorrow we will kiss each other goodbye."

She noticed the goblet on the table in front of her. "I think you need this more than I do. Ah, but it isn't full enough. Let me top it off."

She hobbled into the pantry and emerged soon after, holding the goblet in front of her. "Drink," she said, handing me the goblet. "It will make you feel better."

I didn't want to drink it. I didn't want to drink or eat anything. I was condemned, and I felt it keenly. I didn't want to go to Our Lady of Fiesole. I would rather have been clapped in irons and divested of my nose.

But Nonna urged the wine on me and, to oblige her, I drained the cup. All of it.

I had never drunk this much wine so quickly before. It had the most extraordinary effect. I felt weary — so weary I could hardly keep my eyes open.

"Tired?" Nonna said. "You'd better go upstairs."

I nodded and struggled to my feet. Emilio put a supportive hand on my elbow as though I were an old woman.

"Help her up," she said to Emilio. Then she stroked my hand and smiled a tired smile. "Rest easy, *cara mia,*" she said to me. "I will see you in the morning."

Chapter Fifteen

I was awakened by banging on the door. I looked around me. For a moment I didn't know where I was — my sleep had been so deep I felt as though I were struggling through a fog. Gradually details registered: I was in my room; Domenica was gone; her bed had been slept in. The bells were tolling at Santa Maria del Fiore, summoning everyone to high mass. It was Easter Sunday and I had overslept.

"Flora!" The banging continued. "Get up!"

I opened the door and there was Emilio, his hands in fists ready to pound the door again.

"What's going on?" I asked, rubbing my eyes.

"Captain Umberto wants you," he said. "Get dressed and come quickly. And Flora: a clean gown. We're going to mass."

I had questions to ask him, but he slammed the door in my face, and all I could do was obey. I wondered what could be so urgent.

When I was finished dressing, I followed Emilio downstairs. Captain Umberto stood in front of the *palazzo* surrounded by a half dozen guards. Where were the rest?

"*Grazie a Dio,* there you are, Flora," Captain Umberto said. "I have need of your services."

"You can have nothing for me to do. Today I have to go embroider underwear and grow old. Or had you not heard?"

"Put that out of your mind for now. This task is of the utmost urgency."

I watched as his eyes darted up and down the street. I'd seen him vicious, I'd seen him addled with love, but I had never seen him this agitated.

"Where," I asked softly, "are Riorio's men?" I felt an unfamiliar dread creep over me.

Captain Umberto nodded. "You have hit upon it. They've been missing since before dawn. Emilio here felt something amiss and had the presence of mind to follow them."

"Riorio himself has gone with the rest of your family to Santa Croce for mass," Emilio said. "But his guard did not accompany them. They shadowed the Medici brothers and are even now going in to high mass at the *duomo*."

The events of the party the night before came crashing

down around me: my conversation with Giuliano; Botticelli's masterwork; Signora de Medici's snub of Domenica.

"We fear your father may have acted foolishly," Captain Umberto said.

"You believe he'd do something at high mass?"

"We must think the worst if we are to prevent it."

"*Allora.* What can I do?"

"Emilio followed Riorio's men to the *duomo* but lost them inside. He was unable to get close to the Medici because . . ."

"I am only a *contadino,*" Emilio interjected. There was no shame in his words; he merely stated fact. At Santa Maria del Fiore, as in other churches, only noblemen were allowed up front. And with the size of Santa Maria del Fiore, Emilio would have to station himself half a league away.

I nodded. "Only a noble can get close to *Il Magnifico.*"

"Emilio will escort you to the *duomo.* Stand as close to the Medici as you can and be ready." So saying, he handed me his *squarcato* — a real blade this time, not a wooden one. Short and square, its heft in my right hand was still substantial.

I put the weapon in my girdle under my dress. Two mounts were brought. I willed myself to breathe as I climbed into the saddle. After all, wasn't this what I had always hoped for? To be of use? To do something more than clear dishes?

One of the men, Piero, handed me up a kerchief to use as a veil. "*Per piacere, signorina.* Be careful," he said. Worry was plastered on his face.

I couldn't remember a time any of these men called me *signorina.* I couldn't remember ever having been anything but Flora. But the title and kerchief were kindly meant, so I thanked him and pinned it to my head. When I was done, Captain Umberto reached up and kissed my hand. "Remember, Flora: you are as good as any of my men. Godspeed."

Around me, the complement of soldiers, Umberto included, bowed low as though I were a princess. "Godspeed, Signorina Flora," they said, crossing themselves. Some even kissed the hem of my dress.

The courtesy impressed and frightened me. I felt as though they were sending me to my death.

Emilio and I galloped the two blocks to the Piazza del Duomo.

The passage between the *duomo* and the baptistery was packed with the liveries of all the best noble clans of Florence. There was the coat of arms for the Strozzi family, the Turnabuoni, the Pitti, and the Riccardi. The servants attending the horses were powdered into ghosthood. The air itself was decorated with brightly colored streamers. And why not? Hallelujah. Christ had risen. It was time for us to emerge from a long winter of fasting and renew ourselves in His triumph over death.

God forgive me, but at that moment I prayed Emilio and I would be as successful as He.

Emilio dismounted first and handed me down. I knew we were in a rush, but there were ushers out front and they were watching. I had to behave nobly. So I lifted my skirt delicately and held myself erect. Emilio and I walked as calmly as we could to the entrance.

"Signorina Flora," an usher said. "*Benvenuto.* We were told your family would be at Santa Croce today."

"I prefer the hell of Father Alberto to the dull heaven of Santa Croce," I said with a conspiratorial smile.

The usher smiled back. "I cannot fault your taste," he said, guiding me inside.

Emilio followed but met with an arm blocking his way. "You," the usher said, holding a kerchief to his nose. "In the gallery."

"I stay with my mistress," said Emilio.

The usher motioned to the gallery. Begone. Emilio shot me a concerned look but I nodded. *Tranquillo, all will be well.*

The first half of Santa Maria del Fiore is like that of a normal church: two rows of pews pointed at the high altar, smaller chapels and confessionals on either side. But several paces toward the high altar, and the heavens themselves opened up underneath the vaulted ceiling of our magnificent dome.

The usher escorted me to the second pew from the front, the one always held in reserve for the Pazzi family, the second richest in all of Florence. I took my place directly in back of *Il Magnifico* and his brother, the hapless Giuliano. They stood; they breathed. All was well. Giuliano even craned his head around and greeted me with a wink.

I looked around but saw no sign of Riorio's men. All I saw was velvet and more velvet.

I muttered a prayer and looked up to the very top of the ceiling. *"Per piacere, Dio.* Give me strength."

Father Alberto stood in front of the congregation, in finely woven white robes with an elaborate gold cross embroidered down the middle. I never would have thought him the same threadbare priest who refused payment for sanctifying a bit of ground.

He had just ended his sermon. His arms were open to all of us, calling the congregation to communion.

Lorenzo and Giuliano went first as befit their station. For four steps all was as it should have been.

Then from the corner of my eye, I caught a flash of black. Five men in dark cloaks drew daggers and descended on the Medici brothers. I heard someone scream. It was me.

Lorenzo and Giuliano had enough time to turn around before they saw their attackers. Giuliano placed himself in front of his brother. "Usurers!" the assassins cried as they descended on the Medici. "Adulterers!"

Around me, women screamed and everyone backed away. The brothers and the assassins were on the altar now — the assassins leaning over the Medici, surrounding them in a sea of black. Their knives came down again and again. The screaming was horrible; the sight of the red knives even worse.

A bejeweled hand stuck out from between the legs of the assassins. The fingers curled and then relaxed. When I saw that hand, it was as though the poison keeping me immobile wore off and I dashed forward. *Giuliano,* I thought. *I have to save Giuliano.* I grabbed the outstretched palm, gave one hard yank, and pulled the body free. Then I dragged a man across the floor, leaving a trail of blood, followed by men in hooded black robes wielding knives. Where was someone to help me?

I saw men beckoning to the left, men with tunics emblazoned with the three *palle* of the Medici coat of arms.

"This way, *signorina!*" they shrieked, beckoning to the bronze doors of the sacristy. *"Subito!"*

But Giuliano was heavy, dead weight — and I was slow. Three black cloaks were upon me before I could close the distance. Hands pulled me away from his body and wrestled me to the floor. I looked up.

Crouched over me was Riorio's oaf who had threatened Nonna and sliced my arm. He held a knife dripping gore. There was a look in his eye, and I realized he had been waiting for an excuse to run me through. I grabbed for Umberto's *squarcato* where it was hidden in my girdle, but I was too slow. I would not be in time to ward off the first thrust.

The blow, when it came, barely scratched my shoulder. I didn't feel a thing, although suddenly I was drowning in a geyser of red, flooding my eyes and giving a salty taste to my mouth. Then the oaf fell forward on me, his throat slashed from ear to ear. Strong arms pushed his weight off me, and then there was Emilio offering me one hand, the other holding his *squarcato* drawn and red.

I looked around for Giuliano and found him — a man cloaked in blood and velvet — crawling toward the sacristy doors. The Medici guard had managed to rush to the altar and had engaged the assassins. Giuliano's progress was too slow. He would never make it.

Emilio and I ran over to him. We each grabbed an arm and finished dragging him to the sacristy doors, where his men took him from us and barricaded the bronze doors in our faces.

Emilio and I were left out in the open. We turned around, ready to defend ourselves, but there was no one left to defend ourselves against. Where a moment ago there was confusion and we could hear nothing for the screaming, now everything was eerily silent. The assassins who hadn't been killed drew back into the crowd. Around us, everyone seemed to be waiting. But for what?

Then we saw the altar. Father Alberto had a man's head in his lap, a man who was lying in a spreading pool of blood. Oh no, I thought. Lorenzo isn't going to make it.

But it wasn't Lorenzo.

All had been confusion not seconds earlier. I had grabbed the hand that seemed in most need, and I had grabbed the wrong one. I had not grabbed my friend, I had grabbed my enemy. And now my friend was bleeding heavily from the stomach — giant red bubbles coming from his mouth. There was at least one bad wound on his neck, more under his robes. He breathed in a sickening rasp, his whole body drawing up with the effort.

I ran to him and pulled away his tunic, counting at least nine wounds. There was one particularly bad one down low, from which something else emerged with blood, something slick. I pushed the slick thing back into his stomach and tried to stanch the blood with my kerchief.

"Help!" I cried. The congregation stood back.

"Help!" I repeated. "We need a doctor!"

Giuliano grabbed my sleeve and struggled to speak.

"*Tranquillo,*" I shushed him, summoning Nonna's most competent expression. "We're getting help. Now you must rest."

He used one finger and beckoned me down toward his mouth. He wanted to tell me something.

I gripped his hand tightly, afraid to let go. I couldn't understand what he was saying but I knew what he was thinking. "Don't worry," I whispered. "I'll take care of your son."

His grip on my hand grew weak; he coughed up a bucket of blood and then fell back. There was no more rasping, no noise from him at all. I had failed.

Above me, Father Alberto made the sign of the cross over Giuliano's body.

No one else moved.

"*Cretini!*" I spat at the congregation. "Why did no one help me? What are you all waiting for?"

I looked around the crowd. They were still as statues — even Lucrezia de Medici. Then, from the back of the crowd, someone pointed upward. "Look! In the choir!"

I followed where the man was pointing. There in the loft above the sacristy stood *Il Magnifico,* bleeding from the neck, but very much alive. Emilio and I had saved him.

At that moment I was sickened by this city and every man and woman in it. I realized why no one had helped me.

They were waiting to see who won.

If Riorio's men had killed both Giuliano and Lorenzo, the crowd would have reviled Lucrezia de Medici and sent for my father at Santa Croce to crown him the new leader of Florence.

But Lorenzo lived, and by living outmaneuvered my father once and for all.

"Sacrilege!" someone in the crowd called. "Murder!"

Giuliano's mother, the formidable Lucrezia, finally grew animated. *"Bambino mio!"* she shouted, pushing forward to her dead son.

A dozen or so came to her aid. "Please, *signora,* let me hold you up."

I was shoved aside.

Father Alberto, unmindful of the mess, took my hand. "Time for you to leave, *signorina,*" he whispered. "This is no place for a maiden."

He did not say Flora. He did not say Pazzi.

Emilio was there as well, pulling at me. "Come," he said. "We have to leave *now.*" Then he whispered in my ear: "It's already done. We have to warn the others."

I nodded and we hurried down the aisle to our horses. I came in a lady; I left a fugitive.

As Emilio pulled me along, I glanced back up to the choir. Lorenzo de Medici was still there, observing the commotion below. He was full of righteous fury. He looked as though he could wield thunderbolts and floods. And I knew now that whatever price the Medici paid for their sins, it was enough. The Medici now had God on their side and their wrath would be terrible.

For a moment, *Il Magnifico* turned his gaze on me, and I was so afraid I quaked as though I hadn't eaten in three days. I awaited a subtle nod like he'd given from the government palace that day in the *piazza*. *There. I will have her blood and the blood of the rest of her kin.*

But he didn't point. With his terrible, wrathful face, he bowed low in my direction, and I understood in that instant that he knew everything. He knew whose daughter I was; he also knew what I'd done for him today. For my part in this morning's events, he was granting me a head start.

Chapter Sixteen

Captain Umberto was waiting for us in front of the *palazzo*. Concern made his face so mixed-up he resembled a stew. "*Madonna!* Flora, what has become of you?"

"She's all right," Emilio said, leaping down. "You were right. We were able to save Lorenzo but we were too late for Giuliano."

Captain Umberto clapped Emilio on the shoulder, but he didn't look proud. He still seemed worried. "You've done well, although I fear this is almost worse than had you stayed home."

A noise grew behind us. A mob was forming and they were coming our way, yelling "traitors!" and "assassins." We pressed ourselves against the wall. As they walked our way we caught sight of a man in the middle, a man wearing black and bleeding from the head.

A couple of citizens glared in our direction. "I wonder who's behind this?" one of them spat.

Another man put a hand on his arm and pointed to me. "Didn't you see what that maid did earlier? 'Tis only by her quick wits that *Il Magnifico* lives."

The first one kept glaring. "For your case, *signorina,* I pray your father had no hand in this. Either way, Signor Valentini shall get to the truth of the matter in the Bargello."

As he walked away, still glaring, all I could do was curtsy in his direction. I was covered in blood, under suspicion of murder, but I was still a noblewoman.

When the mob was out of sight, I kept holding myself erect. Too fast. This was all happening too fast. I whispered to Captain Umberto: "Is *all* my family at Santa Croce?"

"Everyone but you and your nonna," Captain Umberto said.

"Bene," I said. "You must get them out of the city with all haste. Don't even venture to come back here."

"Your father," Captain Umberto whispered, "he is expecting a victory. He will not be easily persuaded to flee."

"That is why you must approach my brother Andrea first. Andrea will listen to reason; my father will listen to Andrea."

Captain Umberto nodded. "But what about you, Flora? You'll come with me, surely?"

"Emilio and I have to stay here and take care of Nonna. *Per piacere,* Captain Umberto. Go now. There is no time."

With that I left him. I had to get Nonna out and quick. I knew it would not be long before Riorio's man gave us up.

"Nonna!" I ran to the kitchen, shouting at the top of my lungs. Nonna wasn't there; the kitchen was cold; no fires had been lit. Everything was still and silent.

Something was not right.

"Nonna!" I called into the pantry. Still nothing. I ran up the back stairs to her bedroom. It was still dark within; the shutters pulled tight against the sun. And there was a peculiar smell: the scent of almonds, so strong and close it made me want to gag. Even as I smelled it, a part of me knew what she had done. I threw open the shutters to let in the outside air.

She was lying fully clothed on top of the bed covers.

"*Grazie a Dio* you're still here," I said. "Come, we have to leave now."

I put a hand on her arm and attempted to nudge her awake. But she didn't move; her arms were cold to the touch and strangely rigid.

I still denied what my senses told me. Not Nonna. God would be cruel indeed to take Nonna away from me now. I'd already seen someone die that morning. I had done my share; surely God would not test me more than that.

But I had seen God this morning, looking down from above, and He looked exactly like Lorenzo de Medici.

I looked into Nonna's face. Her lips were black, her eyes open. Gently, I pulled the lids down and began to cry. I knew that there was no point in running. I had lost everything.

I stroked Nonna's cold hands and noticed she gripped something tightly. I pried her fingers apart and found a letter with my name on it, along with a familiar black-dog ring.

I opened the letter. *"Carissima Flora,"* it began. But I didn't get a chance to read more.

"Flora! Flora!" Emilio called my name and ran up the stairs. He saw Nonna and crossed himself. "Poor soul. I hope that now she can rest."

He stood at her side for one silent moment before grasping at me. "All right, now, let's go."

"Sure," I said. "Help me with her arms."

But Emilio was not working with me. In fact, he seemed to be working against me, pulling my hands away, urging me toward the door. "Come, Flora, it's too late for her, just as it's too late for Giuliano. She would not want you to linger."

I wrenched myself away. "I won't leave her."

"She's already gone, Flora," he said, growing impatient. "Now come on."

"No," I said, and pushed him away.

He stumbled two steps backward. "Very well," he said. And went back down the stairs. I didn't hear him come back up; I especially didn't hear him raise a heavy pan and bring it down on the back of my head. All I saw was Nonna's face and then I was slipping. I reached to grab and hold onto her but already I was falling away.

~⊛~

When I came to I was lying on my side in a meadow. I jerked my face out of tall grass, and a cool breeze caressed my cheek. I felt the back of my head. There was a lump there the size of a turnip.

Around me, two horses grazed. Where was I? Then I saw Emilio a short distance away, standing on a summit, pacing back and forth, back and forth. He looked in the opposite direction, down toward the city. He chewed his fingernails as he paced.

We were by his sister's grave in Fiesole.

I had to get back. I didn't belong here, where the horses grew fat on tall grass and the spirit of Emilio's sister stroked our faces. This was a place of peace, and I was still at war.

I crept quietly toward the horse but not quietly enough. Emilio turned around, saw me, and tackled me to the ground.

"I have to go back!" I kept saying as I scratched at his face. "I have to go back!"

"You can't go back!" he said, wagging his finger. "Don't you understand? It's not just Nonna. *Everybody's* dead."

I stopped struggling. How long had I been out? Could it have happened so fast?

"Are you sure? You saw them?"

There was a lie on the tip of his tongue. I saw it sit there like a fine pearl. But he didn't utter it. "No," he said. "But they will be if they stay in town any longer. We have to trust Captain Umberto. He'll get them out if he can. Our part in this is over."

But it didn't *feel* over. In fact, it didn't feel as though it had even begun.

I didn't like most of my family, but I couldn't just abandon them. And then there was Nonna's body. Medici's men would call her *strega*. They would tear her apart and feed the bits to the dogs.

I had to go back. But how? Emilio would not let me out of his sight. If I even suggested such a thing we'd waste valuable time fighting each other, and he would win. I hated to admit it, but he was the stronger of the two of us. I needed an advantage. A little of Nonna's finesse.

In my mind I worked backward from last night and tried to think of what led us to this point. I remembered Mamma's humiliation, Nonna's secret room, Papa and Count Riorio talking in the library . . . I had it. I had my plot.

"Listen, Emilio," I said. "Papa didn't act alone. He was in league with the pope."

Emilio nodded. "The seal," he said, remembering the letter he delivered that first day he was with us.

"The pope sent an army to help him. Even now they are at the Porta Romana in the south of the city. Captain Umberto doesn't know about them. It's all up to you. You must ride quickly and intercept the pope's army. Tell them what happened. Get them to come to the *palazzo*. It's their only chance."

Emilio shook his head. "I won't leave you. I have to get you to the convent. You'll be safe there. Then, in a couple of days, I'll go back to the *duomo*. I'll get the purse we kept with Father Alberto. We'll go north to Milan — or even farther. We'll go to Venice and book passage aboard a ship, the way you wanted."

"Look at me," I said, grabbing his shoulders. "Who do you think needs more help? Me? Or them?"

He said nothing but neither did he whack me on the back of the head. I was making progress.

I continued: "They're still in danger. Captain Umberto is good, but he can't hold off the whole city."

Emilio still said nothing. So I pressed him further. "Come on, Emilio. Didn't you swear to protect us? *All* of us?"

He closed his eyes. I awaited the lecture about how I shouldn't do this or that. But it never came. "Yes, but I don't love the others," he said in a voice just above a whisper.

His words passed over me like a breeze. For a moment then, I looked at my friend, really looked at him, and I saw Emilio for what he had become. All the things I thought defined him: spindly, foul-breathed; they were not the measure of him. Signor Botticelli would be ashamed of me. I had been looking for beauty in the wrong things. The boy whose arms I gripped was no longer spindly; his breath was fresh as mountainous air. And his eyes, the way they looked at me now — they were soft as velvet, and still they made me shake in a way I didn't understand.

Perhaps . . . no, I couldn't think about him that way now. He was my friend, not my swain. Besides, I had to get down off this mountain. Nonna was still down there.

Emilio snapped out of his trance and looked around, suddenly animated. He squeezed my hand. "Do you still have your *squarcato*?" I nodded. "*Bene*. Go straight to the convent and wait there for me. If anyone tries to stop you, use your weapon. Do you understand, Flora? I'll come get you in a couple of days. *Do not go to Venice alone*."

Then I looked my best friend in the eye and I lied like a Pazzi. "I'll be at the convent. I promise."

He mounted his horse and galloped away. I watched him until he was nothing more than a speck of dust.

I tried to convince myself that I would see him again. It's just a little space, I told myself. I needed the time to retrieve Nonna's body and then I would come back. I would be where he told me to be. The two of us would ride away together and I would be happy.

Still, watching him go left a foul, poisonous taste in my mouth, and I knew that I had seen the back of him for all eternity, that all my chances for happiness rode away with him.

Allora. Nothing to be done about it now. I had a task to perform.

What I did next was something I'd rehearsed a hundred times in my dreams. The only difference was I imagined doing this to steal *out* of the *palazzo*. Now I needed to steal back in.

I took Captain Umberto's *squarcato* out of my girdle and cut the hem of my dress until it was the length of a tunic. I brought the blade up to my head.

The chances were good that the Medici army was already at the *palazzo*. I wouldn't be able to get in the door, let alone up to Nonna's room, if people recognized me as one of the family. The only way I could get in was as someone else, a piece of riffraff.

I pulled a hank of hair in front of my face and cut it off. Then more, and more, until I felt a chill on my neck. When I was done my hairline felt ragged, but I didn't care. It didn't have to be clean.

I looked down at the dress I'd torn into a tunic. Underneath the dirt and grass, Giuliano's blood had dried to an earthen brown. I hoped I would just look dirty. I grabbed a handful of soil and spread it over my face.

I walked the remaining horse down the narrow path to Fiesole's town square. I looked at my reflection in a well. It was not a perfect disguise but it would have to do. At least I should be able to get back to the city without being recognized.

I mounted up and rode home.

Chapter Seventeen

Once inside the city I slowed my horse to a trot. I didn't want to look as desperate as I felt. Up and down the streets people leaned out of windows, good people whose faces were transformed into snarls from outrage. They shook their fists and barked news to one another across narrow streets. I heard my family's name. *Murder. Treason. Sacrilege.* I hunched over and prayed no one recognized me.

There was no one on the bench outside our kitchen, so I slipped in as quietly as I could. Inside was evidence of a struggle. Sacks of flour were open and spilled on the floors, turning them white; kettles rolled this way and that. Two troughs of flour ran from the hearth to the courtyard door, as though someone had been dragged by the hair. I followed the furrows and looked out.

The Medici troops had arrived — more than twenty men with the symbol of the *palle* on their tunics. One stood on a bench and read a proclamation. He was a skinny, narrow man. I remembered him from earlier that morning at the *duomo*. He was the one who had urged me on to the sacristy. *This way, signorina.* And even earlier, he was the one who, many months before, had cut a woman's nose from her face in the Piazza della Signoria.

I couldn't hear all of what he said, but this much I did catch: "... and furthermore the coat of arms of the Pazzi family shall be stripped throughout the town, the contents of the bank forfeit. The women in this traitorous nest of vipers shall never be allowed to marry. And as for the men" — he glared at where Papa and Renato and Andrea stood — "your lives are worth nothing. From this moment on you breathe on the sufferance of Lorenzo de Medici, and he is not inclined to mercy. I would take this opportunity to say goodbye to your loved ones, which is more than *Il Magnifico*'s poor murdered brother was able to do."

Captain Umberto and our guard stood between the Medici troops and my family. Behind them I caught a glimpse of the rest. No, this couldn't be. They were all there: Papa, Mamma, Renato, Andrea, Niccolo, Galeotto, Giovanna, Domenica. Papa leaned on Andrea for support — not Renato.

Renato stood a little apart, with the rest of my brothers.

He looked as though he were about to cry. He kept rubbing his hands together, and I realized: this was the first time I'd seen him completely stripped of his rings. Mamma leaned on no one.

Then two of the Medici men brought forth the Botticelli Madonna.

I wanted to look away, but I forced my eyes to stay on the delicate painting. I couldn't bear to see anything happen to it. But then I realized: that wasn't the coming tragedy. My family still breathed but they were about to be torn to pieces and thrown to the dogs. If ever there were a time to act, it was now.

I said a quick prayer for strength, drew my *squarcato,* and stepped out into the light of day.

Captain Umberto was the first to catch sight of me. His eyes narrowed. He shook his head subtly. *Get back.*

I crept back to the threshold but kept my blade drawn. What could he be thinking? We were outnumbered; he needed my help.

I watched his face for another sign. His eyes flicked upward, toward Papa's library. At first I didn't know what he wanted me to do, then I remembered Nonna's secret room. That was where he wanted me. That was where I would go.

I put the blade back on my belt, slunk back into the pantry, and climbed the rickety stairs to Nonna's room.

Nonna was lying as I had left her, still clutching her ring and the letter with my name on it. "These are heavy times,

Nonna," I whispered. "Perhaps best you don't see them, eh?" I kissed her cold forehead then pried the ring and the note from her unyielding fingers.

For a moment all was peaceful. Suddenly, I heard shouts coming from downstairs. Then clanking of blades being crossed, and finally, shrieks.

I leapt to my feet. *Madonna!* It had begun. I had to go down. I had to help my family.

No. I tightened my hands into fists and stayed. I followed orders like a good soldier. Perhaps Captain Umberto meant to bring the family up here that I might sneak them out the kitchen door, which, when I came through, was still clear.

I unclenched my fists and pressed the bronze dog on Nonna's wall and crouched in her poison room.

Soon enough, shouts came from the library.

"This way!" Umberto's voice cried.

I cracked open the door that led to the library hearth.

Last night's fire had died to embers, so I had a clear view of Captain Umberto running in, holding the hand of Domenica. Only Domenica. Why did it have to be her? Why couldn't he have brought Andrea as well? He shut the library door behind them and barricaded it with Papa's heavy desk. As he moved it, an earthen pitcher fell off and crashed to the floor.

Domenica stood against a wall, crying softly. "We can never be married. We can never be married," she chanted.

"Silenzio, signorina," he said, darting to the fireplace. "We don't have much time. Emilio, are you there?"

What did he mean by calling for Emilio? I opened the door the rest of the way and stepped out.

Captain Umberto looked startled. Then I remembered: I was dressed as a boy. "Emilio?" he said again, then he looked closer. "*Flora?* I would never have known you. *Grazie a Dio,* you're alive. Good thinking disguising yourself. You two have a better chance to escape."

"You two?" I said. "You're coming with us, right?"

"I'm a soldier, Flora," he said. "My duty is clear."

He jerked his head around. *Murderers. Traitors.* The cries were getting closer. He grabbed Domenica's hand and shoved her past me into Nonna's dark room.

"You two stay in here. Flora, close the door on the other side, then take your sister and get out the back. No matter what you hear, don't come out. Do you understand? I can hold them off myself."

"I can stand with you," I said. "Domenica can go on her own. Please, I can fight. You taught me how."

"No, Flora, I beg you. Stay here with your sister. Take her away. You're her only chance."

I looked over my shoulder at where my sister was crouched in the dark room, her eyes empty, her senses addled. She was useless. She would never get away on her own. I had to help her, though I didn't want to. I wanted her to stay here, crouched in the dark, while I fought in the open next to Captain Umberto. That was the way things were meant to be.

"*Bene,*" I said, resigned. "Stand tall. This is a dark day, but you have God on your side, I know it."

Captain Umberto smiled an open and warm smile. It was almost the kind of smile I used to dream about but not quite. There was love in it but not the kind I wanted. "Bless you, Flora. You are a good girl." With that he kissed my hand, then slammed the door quickly.

There was clattering in the hearth, and when I touched that wall again it was hot. He had stoked the fire.

Whack! Whack! Someone was taking an ax to the library door. Despite what Captain Umberto told me, I opened the fireplace door a crack. The blaze was roaring now. But I saw his figure beyond the dancing flames. His sword was drawn, his knees bent, his face as vicious as a lion's. There was another *whack!* and the Medici soldiers were through.

The first two didn't even make it over Papa's chair. Captain Umberto skewered them within seconds. But more soldiers climbed over, and more and more. They forced Captain Umberto backward into the room.

He fought with everything he had — pounding men's heads hard onto the marble floor, hurling another out the leaded glass window. Such speed and grace, even though he had on his face the look of the beast that I'd seen that day when Riorio's goon threatened Nonna.

Then more soldiers entered — including the one who read about forfeit in the courtyard. This one seemed more practiced than the others. He waited until Captain Umberto's attention was turned to someone else, then drew his sword and swung it in a perfect arc. My hero's head came off his body and rolled across the floor, a heavy thing.

I closed the door quietly and slouched against a wall. I was going to be sick. "Oh my God," I whispered.

Nonna had said the night before that there came a time when we all must grow up. But she was wrong about one thing — my time didn't come then, it came now. As long as Nonna and Captain Umberto were around, protecting me, protecting us all, I was free to behave the way I wanted. Now there was no one between us and the outside world. The outside world was here, within our walls.

From the library I heard more voices. "Check his pockets," said one. "Take what you find. The rest is now the property of Lorenzo de Medici. If you must keep something for yourselves, make sure you're discreet."

I crept backward and tugged the hem of Domenica's dress. "What's happening downstairs?" I whispered.

"We can never get married," she repeated. I wanted to slap her from here to the Holy Lands.

"Come on, Domenica, I'm trying to help. Now tell me: How many are left in the courtyard? Is there anyone in the kitchen?"

I heard footsteps, this time coming from the other side of the closet, Nonna's room.

"Come on," said a deep voice. "It's just the maid's quarters. Let's go find the good stuff."

"Well, will you look at this. It's the *strega*."

"She's already dead. We're wasting time."

"No, we're not. I'm sure *Il Magnifico* will be able to find a use or two for the mother of that traitor Pazzi. He'll make it worth our while."

Then there was light on my face and I let loose a scream that had nothing to do with God. I leapt out of the closet with my *squarcato* drawn. I heard it squish first and then crunch as I drove it into a man's chest. A warm liquid spurted up and hit me in the eyes.

Someone jumped me from behind. I kicked and clawed but couldn't shake this second man off. So I slammed him against the wall. I slammed again and again until I broke free. The man behind me crumbled to the ground holding his head. He was stunned but not for long. I yanked the hilt of my blade from the first man's chest and plunged it into the chest of the second one. When it was buried to the hilt, I swiveled it around. I didn't want this man to have anything left inside him.

When it was over I pulled Domenica from the dark room. "Come on," I said. "We're getting out of here."

I went over to the bed and began to pull the black dress off Nonna's cold, marbled body. *"Mi dispiace,"* I said. I was not as gentle as I would have liked. I was a soldier with a job to do. Right now my job was getting Domenica to safety.

"What are you doing?" Domenica asked as I yanked Nonna's dress over her head.

"We won't get far with you dressed like that," I told my sister. "Take your gown off and put this one on. And try to slouch."

Domenica did as I said, all the while staring at the bodies of the Medici looters.

"What's become of you, Flora?" she muttered. "What's become of your *hair*?"

I didn't respond. I was grateful that she had her senses back but had no time for her silliness.

At last I managed to work Nonna's dress all the way off and over her head. I threw it to Domenica, who stood shivering in the corner. Nonna had a clean linen shift on underneath, so I didn't have to worry about shrouding her.

Domenica in a threadbare black dress still looked like Domenica. Still shiny and delicate. Hers, like mine, was an imperfect disguise. I only hoped it would be enough.

I threw Nonna's body over my shoulder. I staggered under the weight but I didn't crumple.

Per piacere, Dio, I prayed, *just let the horse be where I left him. I'll manage the rest.*

Domenica and I tiptoed down the stairs and into the pantry. I pushed open the kitchen door. Graziella was there, seated on the floor with her legs out in front of her. She was gorging herself on everything in sight — meat, cheese, Nonna's oranges. She looked up and saw us emerge. "MURDERERS!

TRAITORS!" she called, summoning the Medici army while smiling a wicked smile.

I ran to the door with Nonna's body, but Domenica paused long enough to kick Graziella in the face with her dainty embroidered slipper. It wasn't a forceful kick, but it was enough to make Graziella stop yelling for a moment.

"*Andiamo*," Domenica said when she caught up with me. There was a glint in her eyes that almost pleased me.

Outside I discovered the horse tethered where I left him. A few citizens were gathered by the patients' bench, tracking us with their eyes. They didn't make a move. I threw Nonna's body over the horse's back and helped Domenica up behind her. Then I mounted behind Domenica.

As I seized the reins, two men with sticks and rocks stepped forward. "I know that girl. She's a Pazzi. Let's show the world what Florentines do to murderers."

Then a man with a leather apron held them back. He was Orazio, the goldsmith who had sat with me at dinner only last night. "*Aspetta*," he said gently. *Wait.* It was a quiet gesture, but it worked. The surly man didn't press forward. The others held back as well. I wanted to thank him, but I couldn't waste time, so I merely nodded.

I snapped the reins once and we were gone.

❧

The ride back up the hill was uncomfortable. And although Nonna's body was small and Domenica slight, there were three of us on the back of one small horse. I felt as if at any moment I would fall over backward and kiss the road. But I didn't. And the horse kept his gallop all the way up to Fiesole and past it, about five miles to the convent.

I rolled off the horse and landed on my feet.

I banged on the iron gate. A sister with a deeply wrinkled face in a wimple opened the grille. With one glance she took in everything, my half-witless sister, my blood-stained tunic. "What ails you, *signor*?" she asked kindly. When she opened her mouth I noticed she had practically no teeth in her head.

I wondered who she was talking to, then remembered that I was a *signor* now.

I glanced down at myself. I was wearing a fresh coat of blood. No mistaking this for dirt.

"There's been an accident," I said in a low voice. "My sister needs sanctuary."

She glanced past me to where the horse stood. Domenica was still seated on his back, Nonna draped in front of her.

"What's wrong with the old woman?" she asked.

"She's dead."

The nun looked me up and down again. "I didn't do it," I said. "At least not this one." I wondered if I would ever be able to perfect the art of diplomacy. With my hasty words I doomed us. I just knew it.

She studied me again. Finally she produced a set of keys from her girdle, and the iron door clanged open. "I think you'd better come in," she said. "I am Suor Arcangela. I bid you welcome."

I led the horse inside the convent walls and helped Domenica down. I trundled her to a bench under an olive tree, amidst the neat rows of onions and peas. Suor Arcangela offered her a ladle of well water. More nuns emerged from the refectory.

"We can never get married," Domenica said again as she sipped the water. Her eyes were glazed. I feared she would never recover her right mind.

Someone brought the horse into the courtyard as well, and gentle hands pulled Nonna's body down. One nun made the sign of the cross over her. Another caressed her cold cheek. They would take care of Nonna. If I accomplished nothing else today, I accomplished this.

Suor Arcangela came up to me with another ladle of water. I thanked her. My hands shook as I brought the water to my lips and gulped so fast I spilled half of it down my shirt.

"Slowly, now," she said easily.

When I was done I handed the ladle back to her and forced myself to breathe. I liked this space, I decided. I didn't know what I had expected, but it wasn't this. There were no fountains, no delicate roses. Just neat rows of vegetables and herbs. It wasn't an elaborate garden but it was enough. Until today I'd never known what *enough* looked like.

As I sat there I began to stop shaking. Suor Arcangela came and sat next to me.

"I've misjudged you," I said. "I've never been here. I thought it might be like a prison."

"There are those who need our kind of prison," Suor Arcangela said. She nodded to where Domenica sat staring blankly ahead. "And you, *signor*? Can you not rest with us a piece?"

I shook my head. "I have to go back. There are more."

Suor Arcangela nodded in Domenica's direction. "Like that one?"

"I fear they're more like my blessed nonna," I said.

She crossed herself and kissed a rosary that was hanging around her neck. "I shall pray for you, *signor*. *Allora*. I thought you might need this." She drew from her habit a clean shirt and offered it to me. "There is a corner over there. You can change without being observed."

"Grazie," I said, and began unbelting my own bloody tunic.

My *squarcato* clattered to the ground, along with Nonna's black-dog ring and her letter. The letter had a bloodstain on it; the ring was unmarked. I picked it up and offered it to the nun.

"Here," I said. "For the burial. And for my sister's keep."

She curled my fingers around the ring in my palm and pressed it back on me. "I do not need payment to do my Christian duty. You say that others need your help. Bring them here. We will care for them."

And I knew she would.

I took my ring and letter and changed behind an olive tree. Then I drew up a bucket of well water and splashed my face and arms. When I was done rinsing, the water in the bucket was dark pink.

Even though time was still precious, I had one more task before leaving.

I wished I didn't have to talk to Domenica. Ever. But leaving without saying goodbye didn't seem right. Not after what we'd been through.

So I sat next to her on the garden bench. Her eyes still hadn't focused; her hands played with her hair. "You'll be safe here," I said. "Emilio will come in two days. He'll know what to do."

"What about you?" she said, her eyes suddenly alert. "Why can't *you* come back for me?"

But I was plotting again. Emilio was as fast as the Roman god Mercury. He would have reached the pope's troops by now. They might already be at the *palazzo*. If all went well, my family might yet be saved. Perhaps I was just going back to reassure myself.

"It'll be fine, Domenica. You'll see. I'll be back tonight with the rest."

They're fine, I told myself. *Emilio's there.* But no matter how often I repeated it part of me knew I'd already used my luck getting Nonna and Domenica out. I remembered the gurgling noise Giuliano made as he struggled for his last breath; I remembered how Captain Umberto's head sounded heavy as a cannon ball rolling across the library floor. I re-membered the gathering mob outside the kitchen and how two of them wanted to get at us but Orazio held them back. *Aspetta*. There was only one man with a quiet word to keep the crowd from attacking. He gave us an instant — now my instants were all used up.

"My dresses, my jewelry," Domenica said, still fussing with her hair. "The Medici have taken everything." Tears appeared in her eyes. "I heard the decree. They want us wiped out. They're going to kill our brothers and father. You and I they'll let live, but we can never get married so we can never produce an heir."

To me, this didn't seem like such a big tragedy. I'd never planned on getting married, so I didn't miss it now. This was something she would have to contemplate on her own.

"Flora," she said. I turned around. She stood up and brought a hand to fuss with my own jagged hairline. "If you come back here, we might yet be well together. Your hair will grow. I will show you how to arrange it. And I sew a straighter seam than you do. I could make us both dresses. If you come back I will take care of you. You will be my little sister."

It was a gracious offer, and the look on her face was one I'd seen only in my dreams. Domenica was offering me acceptance. And I realized it wasn't the leaving I always dreamed of, the adventure, the fortune earned — but the embrace. The one Domenica was offering me now.

"*Sorella mia,*" I said, grasping her hands. "That sounds like heaven."

The nuns around us pretended not to stare. They heard her call me *Flora* and *sister* and speak to me of gowns and hairstyles. They knew a little of the deception I practiced upon them.

I mounted my tired horse, focusing on little things: the blisters on my fingers from gripping the reins, the gray mane in front of me. I thought perhaps if I just noticed the little things, the bigger things would take care of themselves.

I kneed my mount and rode out of the courtyard.

"Addio, signorina!" Suor Arcangela called, closing the gates behind me. "Godspeed!"

Then I galloped away, leaving the girl behind.

Chapter Eighteen

I returned to the city at sunset. This time there was no slipping through — the crowds started at the city gates. These people were not leaning out of windows for news — they were debauched revelers. The whole city was like a carnival: people staggered through the streets, shouting *"Palle! Palle!"* The Medici coat of arms became a call to war. These upright citizens carried *our* jugs of wine, juggling *our* silver plates and kettles and hoarding *our* bits of cloth. Had everyone in the city of Florence been looting my house? Take it and welcome, I thought. It is your due. Just leave me my family.

I got off my tired horse at the edge of the city, afraid if I came any farther someone would steal him too. There was foam around his gray muzzle. I should have left him at the convent. I whispered to him that he had been a good horse, a fine horse, then I slapped him on his way. I would not be getting away this time.

I threaded through the crowds to the kitchen entrance of the *palazzo*. No army here. Just looters. They crushed around the kitchen door and conked one another on the heads if they thought someone had something better. I tried to push my way through them, but they pushed back. "I was here first!" people shouted, their eyes narrow with greed. They were no better than my father.

Emilio's there, I muttered. *Everyone is safe.* At least no one recognized me yet. I would make my way to the pope's army, who must be at the front of the *palazzo,* and together we would restrain the crowd and protect what was left of my family.

At the front only shock awaited me.

There was no papal army. Everywhere I looked there seemed to be uniforms with the three balls of the Medici coat of arms. *Palle. Palle. Palle.*

"Death to the traitorous Pazzi!"

"We'll show him how we handle assassins in Florence!"

Where was Emilio?

A cheer arose. There was some kind of spectacle coming out of our front entrance. I was too far back in the crowd to see well, but I did see my father emerge with a rope around his neck and a black hole where his right eye used to be.

Madonna! I was wrong: everyone was not safe, least of all my papa. He was in so much pain he couldn't even cry out. He swayed on his feet, held up by the Medici soldier who killed Captain Umberto. People pelted him with rocks and fruit and clubbed him with heavy sticks, but he didn't seem to feel the blows.

I pressed forward but the crowd pressed me back. They were making way for four horses brought to the front. I didn't understand. Why four horses? If my parents were to be carted off to the Bargello, surely they could just walk?

I tried to make myself as slippery as an eel and squeeze through the crowds, but I made no progress at all.

Papa's head disappeared, and the next thing I heard was horrendous screaming as the four horses were encouraged in different directions. That noise! Why didn't they stop it? I felt ill. That was my papa screaming so loud. And why? What were they doing to him that was so horrible? He hadn't seemed to have that much life left in him.

Then one of the horses trotted past me dragging a human arm behind it.

They had pulled Papa apart.

I swayed on my feet. Around me the crowd went wild. People cheered loudly. *"Forza! Forza!"* Jugs of wine passed freely from one set of hands to the next. *Cretini.* What kind of people thought this was entertaining?

At the *palazzo* entrance, a Medici soldier held my father's bald head up to the crowd, still dripping gore from the neck. There was no body attached to it. I forced myself not to look away. What bothered me wasn't the blood so much, but the fact that the head was uncapped and now everyone could see what he'd tried so hard to conceal during his life. I wanted to wrap that head and protect it, the way I'd protected Nonna's body — even though I knew it didn't matter anymore. He couldn't feel shame. All I could do for my father now was pray for his soul. So I did.

God forgive him, I implored. *He was wrong to plot as he did, but he was my father and I loved him. Accept him into heaven as he never accepted me.*

Then the chanting resumed and they brought my brother Renato forth. "No!" I shouted, trying to be heard over the throng. I tried again to elbow my way through the crowd with as little success.

I cried and reached out — not for Renato (God forgive me) — but because I knew if they were going from oldest to youngest, Andrea would come after him.

No. Not Andrea. No one deserved to be torn apart by horses, but especially not him. He was no conspirator. I had to save him.

The horses were brought again, pieces of my father still dragging behind them. Renato saw them and went crazy with fright. He thrashed harder than a live eel.

"No!" I yelled. "He is innocent!"

No one seemed to hear me, they were chanting so loudly. Even if they had, they wouldn't have known that I was not talking about Renato.

Everyone cheered and wanted a better look. Next to me a man put a young boy on his shoulders so he could see. I reached out and pulled him off.

"What are you doing?" The man grabbed his son away from me.

"*Per piacere, signor,* this is no sight for a child."

"Good," he said as he shoved me away. "Maybe he'll remember this. I want him to know what we Florentines do to traitors."

The man put his child back on his shoulders. The child laughed and clapped and patted his father on the head. I doubted he'd still be clapping in a moment.

As I watched, the child seemed to jump up and down on his father's shoulders. But it wasn't him. My vision blurred. Darkness pressed in on the corners of my eyes. Red specks like cannon fire erupted on the back of my lids. *I had to get to the front of the crowd.*

But no matter who I pushed, there was someone larger and stronger pushing back.

Just then the goldsmith appeared and put an arm under my elbow. "Please, *signor,*" he said, pulling me out of the crowd just before everything went black. "You are not well."

"I'm fine," I said, jerking my arms away.

"What a sissy, eh?" I heard him say to the crowd as I toppled forward. "This one can't stand the sight of blood."

Once again the goldsmith saved me. He grabbed my arm and dragged me to an alley. I staggered to my feet, eager to get back. "Easy now," he said, "you've had a shock."

He tried to support me but I elbowed him away. I made it about two paces, too, until I leaned over and retched into the street. Along with mud and horse dung, I threw up all that was left of my pride.

Orazio patted my back as I heaved. "What do you call youself, *son?*" he said pointedly.

I told him the first name that came to mind.

"It isn't safe out here, Emilio," he said. "We have to get off the streets."

"*Grazie,* Signor Orazio."

"*Prego,*" he said, his eyes darting around us.

Just then a new cry ripped the air. *"Delphine!"* I heard some men yell, using our coat of arms as a rallying cry. From the direction of the *duomo* six men came running wielding weapons.

At last, I thought. The pope's army has arrived. All would be well.

But all wasn't well. From where I stood I could see that the men who had called *"Delphine!"* weren't an army, they weren't even the remnants of an army. They were just six citizens wielding rocks and scythes. I remembered one or two faces from Nonna's kitchen door. There was one man with a hare-lip, another dragging a withered leg. It was an army of invalids. "Don't," I whispered. "You're going to get slaughtered."

They made it a few steps closer to Renato than I did, but they were swallowed by a crowd. For every voice shouting *"Delphine!"* there were ten shouting *"Palle!"* The Medici crowd swallowed up the few souls within seconds. Over and over I watched kicks and blows being delivered and more daggers coming down again and again.

This morning I thought I'd only have to journey through hell once. How many more people would I have to watch get ripped apart? Where was Emilio?

Behind me, the goldsmith was pulling on me. "It's time to take your own advice, *signorina!*" he said, more forcefully this time. "If we stay here we'll be seen and you'll get slaughtered."

But I barely heard him. "We need an army," I said. "I have to get to Porta Romana."

I shook away from his grasp and ran to the other end of the alley — toward the Arno. Toward Porta Romana on the other side. I had to find Emilio and get the pope's army. *Madonna!* When I caught up with that boy I would never forgive him for being so late. He was as lazy as Graziella.

It took me so long to go a short distance. I'd never traveled alone before through the streets, and they were narrow and crowded. I had to cross the Arno, but I couldn't see the

Arno. At last the street I was on opened into the Piazza della Signoria, and from the *piazza* I could see a sliver of blue.

When I reached the river I picked out the Ponte Vecchio and ran across that. From there it was straight to the statue of Mercury that marked the southern edge of our city. I ran to it as though I were being chased.

When I touched the statue I stopped and looked around. There were a few people and carts coming and going. Normal traffic. There was no army. There was no Emilio. There was no one but me. I ran along the road to the south, calling, "Emilio! Emilio! I'm here!" I saw no one. I tried the neighborhoods to the east and west. Still no uniforms; no army. Hardly any people, either. The whole city must have been at our *palazzo,* picking over our possessions and our bones.

After what seemed like hours, I came back to the statue and sat down, resting my head in my hands.

There was no army.

"Come on, you *cretino*! We have to get back! We have to save Andrea!" I cried, but I was talking to the sky.

Suddenly, I began to shake and I couldn't stop. The sky spun around, whipped by a strong wind, and I sank down right there, under the statue of Mercury, because suddenly I understood.

There was no army. Zephyrus had caught up with me. It was not my fate to save my family — it was my fate to be the one who escaped.

Maybe the army was never here. Count Riorio could have lied about them to Papa that day he made his threats. But if he were so eager to oust the Medici and rule Florence himself, wouldn't he have needed the pope's army too?

There was another possibility I didn't want to face. Perhaps they were here but Emilio never arrived. The pope's men thought the coup had been called off and by now were back in Rome kissing rings and drinking sacramental wine.

I had watched Emilio from Fiesole. I had watched him until he was almost here. What could have happened? Then I remembered the cheering of the crowd as they tore my father apart, the way they hoarded pieces of our silver and called everyone *traitor*. The whole city hated us and anyone that had anything to do with us. Killing us had become a sport, and Emilio had been wearing his tunic with the Pazzi *delphine* on it. The rest wasn't difficult to guess. Someone cut his head off and then rummaged through his pockets for a painting or a bit of cloth.

Not Emilio. It couldn't be. If something happened to him it was my fault. He could have gotten away. But I sent him back. With my lie I killed that boy, my first and only friend.

"Emilio." A rough hand was on my back. I looked up, startled. Where? I only barely understood that it was the goldsmith, and he was talking to me.

I was Emilio now.

"You should not stay here. People are beginning to stare," he whispered. And it was true. I'd been so cocooned in my own grief that I hadn't noticed what a scene I made, huddled here on the ground, cascading tears. Everyone who passed looked at me openly, some of them for a little too long.

"Come on, son," the goldsmith said, a little louder now. "I'm sorry we quarreled. Let me take you home."

I didn't push him away. I didn't do anything. I let him support me as we went back the way I came, slowly this time. Over the bridge. Through the Piazza della Signoria. All the while he muttered for the sake of passersby: "My boy the sissy. The events of the day have left him overexcited. You'll have to develop a thicker skin, son, if you want to survive in this town."

Finally, we came back to the Via dei Balastrieri but stopped short of our *palazzo*. Orazio ushered me in a building, and I made it over the threshold before the smoke and the heat made me choke.

Surely, I thought as I pitched forward, this man has just calmly ushered me into hell.

Chapter Nineteen

I awoke swatting at something crawling on my head.
I was lying on a pallet of straw in a curtained room. A flea
jumped out of the straw and onto my elbow. I flicked it off.
They were crawling all over the pallet, and apparently all over
me as well.

I took a deep breath. My throat was dry and scratchy as
parchment. The air around me was hot and close, but I was
able to squeeze some into my chest.

I leapt up and parted the curtains. Beyond was a small
room with rough wooden floors swept clean. Maestro Orazio
sat at an oak table scored with burn marks. His hands, the size

and color of charred sausages, were wrapped around a ceramic mug.

The woman who sat next to him was a stout woman of middle age. She wore a short-sleeved dress under an apron: brown over white. She was not as red as her husband, but she still wasn't the kind to smear goat's-milk paste on her face. She stood over the hearth stirring a kettle of something and it smelled good. Not elaborate like eels or pheasants — maybe a kind of soup. I was hungry although I didn't want to be.

"Are you sure, Orazio? Is there no other way?" this woman said.

Orazio shook his head. "We owe it to Signora Cenesta. It may not be as dangerous as you think, Maria. They say the *boys* of the Pazzi family are all accounted for. You saw as well as I did that this one is no boy."

"What do you mean the boys are all accounted for? Where are they?" I spoke up.

The woman looked at me and then exchanged a glance with her husband. She stood and offered me her chair. "You'd best sit down," she said.

I remained standing. "Thank you for your hospitality, but I have to find out what happened to my brothers. There may still be time."

Maestro Orazio and his wife exchanged a glance.

"It is too late. They are beyond your reach."

"Every one of them? All dead? Even Mamma?"

"Your mother is cloistered in a small room in your old *palazzo*. They will not kill her, but she will not be allowed her freedom."

I tried to muster a measure of pity for my poor, stripped mamma, but found I didn't have much. She still breathed; many of the others did not thanks in part to her greed.

"And my brothers? Are they all dead as well?"

"I gather you have two brothers in the clergy. They will be allowed to live."

"And the rest?"

Neither said anything.

"Please, you must tell me: is there any hope at all?"

"Orazio," his wife said, putting a hand on his arm. "This one will not stay put. You'd best open the shutters."

Orazio seemed to age twenty years as he stood there, but he nodded in assent. "Stand back," he told me. "Your disguise seems good enough, but we don't know. Best you not be seen."

Harsh sunlight filled the room. It had been sunset the last I remembered — almost a full day had passed.

I shielded my eyes from the glare; then, slowly, as they became accustomed to the brightness, I inched forward and looked outside.

We were on the second floor of a building on the same street as our *palazzo,* only a few blocks closer to the Arno and on the opposite side. From where I stood I could barely make out our *palazzo* walls. Down below, the streets were in chaos.

I could no longer make out anyone calling slogans, like *delphine,* or *palle;* it just seemed like a citywide tavern brawl. I don't think the citizens knew what they were fighting about. People were hitting each other, pelting each other with rocks, shouting insults. It all sounded like one giant cry. Then Maestro Orazio nudged me and pointed at a spot above the crowds that was level with our eyes.

I had never seen the Bargello prison up close. Andrea always shut the curtains tight on the carriage when we went past. I'd always wondered why.

And now I knew. Corpses were strung from its walls, blackened things with hands tied behind their backs and jackdaws picking at their eye sockets — the ones that still had hands — and heads. There were little bits of people hanging as well — an arm here, a leg there. At the beginning of this display was a head on a pike.

How did people even identify the remains of these poor souls? How would anyone know to claim that bald head?

My blood went cold. *Madonna.* That was my father's head. And next to it, pieces of Renato. There was Galeotto, then Giovanni, and next to him Niccolo. That was my family strung up there as a warning to others.

"How could this have happened?" I said, staring, my mouth agape. "Where was the army?"

"What army?" Signora Maria asked.

"The pope's army. He said they'd be there."

"Who said? The pope?" Maestro Orazio asked.

"No. Count Riorio." Before I was done pronouncing his name, I understood the extent of his betrayal. *"Cretino,"* I muttered.

Maestro Orazio nodded in agreement. "Count Riorio is back in Forli. They say he has barricaded himself in his castle and lives in fear like a coward. I don't know what he promised you, but it is published abroad that he is not a man of his word."

"That's the least of it," I said.

"There was no army," Maria said gently, pouring me a mug of water from an earthen pitcher. "Please. You are not well. Sit down."

I accepted the mug but remained standing. The water was filthy and brown, but I drank it deeply and gratefully, as though it were the nectar of the gods.

In the meantime I kept looking at the grotesque display hanging from the Bargello walls. I counted everyone, twice and three times. There were a few extra body parts. But three of my brothers were missing: Antonio and Lionardo were not there, but they were clergymen as Orazio had said. But there was another body missing.

"Where is Andrea?"

Orazio flashed his eyes in the direction of the prison. "Inside."

I leaned against the windowpane. So my brother had joined the ranks of those piteous souls, whose cries I'd heard from our rooftop, those who had forgotten how to dream.

"Then we have to get him out."

"Nobody comes out of there, Emilio," Maria said, taking extra time, practicing my strange new name. "Unless they're dead."

I looked down at the street and counted the Medici guard in front of the Bargello. I stopped counting at twenty. I could not break in alone. There were only the two people standing next to me to take my part. After what I'd seen, I knew they harbored me at great personal risk.

"*Grazie,*" I said. "I'm very mindful of what you've done for me. Now I have to decide what's next."

Maestro Orazio used a meaty hand to scratch his head. Signora Maria went back to stirring her soup. I had a feeling that their movements were rehearsed, agreed upon in advance. "We have been talking," he said. "Your nonna — rest her soul — once did us a kindness. We had a son many years ago. He coughed black before he was ten years old. We summoned doctors who let his blood and charged us money but didn't cure him. The leeches got fat; our son got thin. Then we sent for Signora Cenesta. She spoke to him so tenderly — wiping his brow. She even sang and rocked him to sleep. Then when he was resting comfortably, she whispered to us that our only child was going to die."

Signora Maria wiped away a tear from her face. I had no

idea how old her tragedy was, but I knew to her it would always be as fresh as mine was today.

"Mi dispiace," I said. "Nonna could be blunt."

Maestro Orazio shook his head. "You misunderstand — she did us a kindness. She didn't give us false hope. Because of her we were able to make him comfortable as he left this life. Because of her we were able to be strong."

Orazio reached into his shirt and pulled out three objects. The first was Captain Umberto's *squarcato.* The second was a bloodstained letter; the third, a ring with a black dog. The seal on the letter was broken.

"These fell out of your shirt when we carried you upstairs earlier. This ring is my handiwork. Forgive me, but I read the letter. I had to know."

I picked up the ring and ran my finger over the now-familiar black dog. "Such intricate work," Orazio said. "I don't make very many of these. May I?" I handed the ring back to him. He popped open a hidden hinge to reveal a small compartment — big enough for a deadly dose of poison, discreet enough that no one would be able to detect if it were dumped in someone's wine or soup.

I took the ring from him. I'd never seen the compartment before, but watching it spring open, it was as though little bits of hidden knowledge had sprung open as well. I brought the ring with its compartment up to my nose knowing before I did what I would smell: almonds. Nonna had either been making a very fine pastry, or she had used this compartment for arsenic.

So now I knew for sure: the black dog was her symbol, a symbol of death. Nonna was a killer, hunched over, laboring in a dark, hidden chamber. And yet I still loved her. I knew that everything Nonna did she did for us. She was no villain: she was a warrior. This ring was her weapon.

"Such a ring has value with certain patrons," Orazio continued. "I would be pleased to buy it from you for twenty florins. It's not much, but it would be enough to buy your passage to Rome, for example . . ."

". . . or Venice," I said.

"*Bene.* Or Venice," he said.

I fell silent. Two days ago I would have taken the offer, but I was a different person then. I was still Flora.

And now, as Emilio, I felt I didn't deserve Venice. I didn't even deserve to dream of it. Men had died around me yesterday. One in my lap; several just out of reach. It made no difference. For all I'd been able to do for them, they might all have been out of reach.

"There's another alternative," Signora Maria said. "You could use it to buy your apprenticeship in the shop, with us."

I looked up at her.

"We've been discussing this," Orazio continued. "They are not looking for any boys, *Emilio.* Your brothers are all accounted for; your father is dead. Your married sisters who live in Florence have been stripped of their possessions and cast out — and so shall your mother be. The news from the *Signoria* is that only two Pazzi daughters are still at large. One of them was seen leaving in the company of a kitchen boy. No one seems to know what happened to the second. No one even knows what she looks like. At least that's what they say. You were visible enough to the right sort. That sort will not tell out of respect for your dear nonna."

After what I'd seen today, I found it hard to believe that anyone would hold back in bringing a member of my family to justice.

Maria apparently agreed. "We don't know that, Orazio," she said, covering his sausage-shaped hand with hers.

"You're right. We don't know, we only suspect. And it's only fair to tell you that there is a substantial reward for information about Lorenza Pazzi. You would have to stay indoors all the time. At least in the beginning. Maybe after the first few months we could let you out for mass."

I said nothing; I fingered Nonna's ring.

Maestro Orazio continued: "It wouldn't be the same, you know. We are not like your family. We don't wear fine clothes here, nor do we dine as well as they did at your house. Some days, when commissions are thin, we don't dine at all."

"And you could never take the place of our lost son," Signora Maria said softly.

"Maria, please, she's been through enough."

"It's important that she know the truth, Orazio. This one is stronger than you think."

Maestro Orazio looked at me from the corner of his eye. "My wife is trying to tell you that you would live with us and dine with us but you would not be ours. We would shelter you to discharge an old debt; nothing more. We owe Signora Cenesta that much."

Maria sighed. "Surely you can understand," she said. "We have lost the person we loved most in the world. We do not want to go through that again ever in this lifetime."

I watched her gently place her hand in Maestro Orazio's, and from seeing the tenderness of the gesture, I knew she was kidding herself.

And yet I could understand how they felt. I had no more goodbyes left in me after today. Better to armor yourself in lovelessness.

"Also," Maestro Orazio said. "The view from here is not so good. Perhaps it would be too much. But you would be of use. Signora Cenesta said you liked to work and that you served them well."

I shook my head. "Not well enough." And although I tried, I couldn't help myself. I sobbed, a ferocious, stabbing sob that began in my belly and slowly came up to my head.

"Allora," Maria said, pushing Nonna's letter toward me. "Let's give this youth some time to consider our offer." She pushed my letter toward me. "Perhaps this will help make up your mind. When you're ready, we'll be in the shop."

"*Carissima Flora,*" the letter began . . .

By the time you get this I will be gone and you will be en route to the sanctuary of the convent. I know it is not your first choice, nor is it mine. At least you will be safe. Your father will not heed my counsel and is determined to act against the Medici.

You have been a good girl. That day I found you in my chamber I saw the questions in your eyes and I told you that someday I would answer them, although I suspect you already know the truth: I am a murderess, Flora. I murdered my husband, I murdered the man who pushed you in the garden. There have been others.

Murder is a mortal sin — not the kind you can reveal in confession. When I die there will be no reprieve for me. I knew this years ago and vowed to help whom I could, hoping my good works would balance the bad. I brewed my atonement from herbs and broth. And not once in the autumn and winter of my life did I purchase yellow orpiment to grind into arsenic. The room you discovered lay shut for years.

And then that ape of a man shoved you.

For now we come to something I should have told you years ago. I love you, Flora. Until you came along I fancied myself all dried out. I tended to the sick and to your brothers and sisters because it was my duty.

You were more than my duty, cara mia. Even when you were a baby you had a way of smiling that drew my heart from my chest. And even now when I saw you standing in front of my chamber, holding the goblet with the arsenic in it, I was scared and I knew you were the one thing I couldn't part with. I thought God himself had come to take you away from me. I was spared that day, but I knew that my luck had ended.

So that is why you are in the convent now, cara mia. You will not make a good nun, but at least you will live. And you don't have to be there forever. Emilio is a good boy. I've seen the way he looks at you and even though you do not look at him the same way, you are both young yet. I've spoken to him and he agrees. He will stay here working with us. I will find a way to get money to him gradually, although not too much. I have seen what too much money does to people. He will come for you when he has enough to make a start.

And now my time is done. I prefer to pick the hour of my leaving rather than endure another moment in the company of your mother. I go to sleep satisfied that you are at least out of danger.

Be strong, cara mia. Stay safe. Zephyrus will pursue you for a while, but I know that, whatever you decide, you will emerge in splendor and bring a new season to the lives of others just as you have brought a new season to mine.

Addio,
Cenesta Pazzi, Your Nonna

I read through the letter again and again until I committed it to memory. Then I cast it on the hearth. My new master and mistress were generous, but such a letter was too dangerous to keep.

When there was nothing left of it but ash, I put on her ring and went downstairs to the hot, smoky forges. Maestro Orazio said I would not be able to go outside. Not for months at a time. That seemed like a suitable penance for me, shut up in here, away from everything green, away from the changing seasons.

Signor Botticelli once said that he didn't stay a goldsmith

because he couldn't stand the smell. Or the heat. Or the burned fingers. He said that to be a goldsmith one had not only to endure beastly working conditions but they also had to enjoy torturing shapeless lumps into works of art. I thought of Ghiberti's bronze gates of paradise, elaborate and beautiful, and I wondered if a person could fashion their atonement from hot metal, the way Nonna brewed hers from herbs and broth.

It was time for me to find out.

Chapter Twenty

Maestro Orazio was wrong about one thing: his shop had the perfect vista. Every morning before I began my labor I leaned outside and counted the bodies strung from the upper stories, a count that increased daily as more were implicated in what they were now calling *la Congiura di Pazzi,* the Pazzi Rebellion. People I'd seen only once, or never seen in my life, were added to my brothers because they did business with us, or supped with us, or even nodded to us on the street. Graziella was the first non-Pazzi, non-Riorio goon to be added to the corpses swinging from the prison walls (they did put some women to death, apparently). Then came an endless line of conspirators: all of Riorio's men (but not Riorio), everyone from our guard, the musicians who regularly performed in the great hall, the footmen, the clerks from the bank. I even caught sight of Francesco, whom Andrea almost fired a month ago for my crimes.

There were more, but I stopped recognizing them after the ancient *contadino* who sold Nonna wild strawberries through the kitchen window. All I knew was this: Andrea's body didn't appear, nor did Emilio's. And while I knew from the talk that Andrea was still alive within the prison walls, I had no hope for Emilio. He would not have left us. He was as dead as my father. I only hoped he was buried somewhere — preferably in one piece.

Orazio's shop also had the perfect vista for me to learn about what was happening in the world outside the city. Notices were posted outside the Bargello as well as fingers and heads. In this way I read about how Pope Sixtus excommunicated Lorenzo de Medici for crimes against the Pazzi family. The pope also imposed an interdict against the whole city. No one could celebrate mass. We were all going to hell, according to him. The interdict didn't affect me. I was already there.

Thanks to Maestro Orazio's vista, I also learned the fate of my mother.

I had been an apprentice goldsmith for about a month. I was learning engraving, spending most of my days crouched over a workbench carving shapes into soft metal. *To G. From E. I love you forever.* From letters I progressed to swirls, ivy, and cherubs. It was a cherub that employed me that afternoon (a cherub who, under my novice's hands, looked like a sack of meal) when I heard a roar coming from outside. I leaned out the window and observed a crowd lining the streets. The roar was the citizens of our city of flowers awaiting some event. I confess by that time I had grown cavalier about the bloodlust. Who is it now? I wondered. My uncle's cousin's tanner's wet nurse?

I stared out the window as the roaring grew louder. The crowds parted long enough for me to see my mother, wearing sackcloth, her hands bound in front of her, being led south through the streets by a Medici guard on a horse. Her head was uncovered, but her posture was unbowed, no matter what she wore, or how many rotten eggs trickled down her face. Had her hair always been so gray?

I heard citizens yell and spit. "Exile is too good for that serpent." "Why should she live in luxury while poor Giuliano is cold in his grave?" "There won't be any luxury for her. She's going to live with her daughter in Naples. King Ferrante won't allow her any comfort — not while the peace talks are so delicate."

Since I had been watching the notices and listening to the talk of customers (few) and passersby (many), I knew that King Ferrante was the one man of consequence in the entire peninsula who was neutral in our conflict. He was friendly with the Medici; he was also friendly with Pope Sixtus; and it was to Naples that *Il Magnifico* had ridden to plead for intervention after being excommunicated. The plan clearly must have worked because the interdict was lifted and Pope Sixtus's Medici brother (his words) was welcomed back into the loving bosom of the church, along with the entire city.

And now, watching Mamma make her way through the streets, her hands bound in front of her, but still proud, I felt my blood boil. I told myself I had no right to be angry. How many times had I wanted to do exactly what everyone else was doing? Swear and hurl things at her? And her: could it hurt her to show a little sorrow, a little shame? She did not deserve to live. I was angry with all of them.

It was at that moment I saw her stumble.

She tried to catch her fall with her hands but wound up on her knees. The Medici guard who was leading her just looked back and yanked her rope hard, as though she were a stubborn goat. She tried to get to her feet but stumbled again. Without thinking I rushed out, forced my way through the crowd that lined the street, and plucked her up. I lifted her by the elbow and brushed the worst of the mud from her lips with my own hands, now blackened from the forges like my master's. At that instant as I looked into her face, she seemed not only old but vulnerable as well. She looked on me with a confused expression, as though she not only didn't know who I was, but didn't even know which way was up. The expression lasted only a moment. Then her eyes narrowed. *"Grazie,"* she said. But she didn't really mean it. Not to an urchin like me.

I let her go. Before she'd even gone two steps I felt a whack on my shoulders. I turned around and wiped what was left of a tomato off my shirt. A middle-aged man positioned himself in front of the crowd, his throwing arm lax, his face twisted up with righteous fury. "What are you doing showing pity to that witch, boy? Are you blind? She's a Pazzi," he spat.

"She's still someone's mamma," I countered in my deepest voice. I was still disguised.

The man smirked. "Not anymore."

I took a lesson from Nonna and stood tall. I didn't swear, I didn't spit, I didn't throw anything back. I kept my voice steady: "All the more reason to show her pity. A good Christian would."

It was a strange moment. I watched as all the rage drained out of that man. It left him shaky and uncomfortable. He took a step back and scurried away, grumbling as though he were a child deprived of a treat. With him gone, I watched my mamma continue down the street unharassed. No one threw anything else at her.

Did I think even once about joining her, taking my rightful place at her side? Going to King Ferrante's court in Naples? A place where I would be comfortable but barely tolerated?

Not even for an instant.

Instead I felt a small measure of freedom. As Mamma walked away from me, I knew I had discharged a debt. She gave birth to me; I allowed her to keep her pride for those few last paces out of town. It was a small accomplishment but it was enough. I was sure Nonna would approve.

Back inside my master was waiting for me. As soon as I stepped over the threshold he closed the door behind me and dealt me a blow that sent me sprawling halfway across the floor. *"Stupida!"* he yelled. "What were you thinking?" I didn't answer him. I crouched where I had landed and wiped the blood from my mouth. I watched him pace back and forth, back and forth. Then, as with the man on the street, the rage seemed to drain from him. He breathed out deeply and offered me a hand up. "Do you not understand, Emilio," he said with forced patience, "that when you did that you not only endangered yourself but Maria and me as well? You could have been discovered. We could be hanged. I know you have little care for your own life, but please think of us before you act next time."

I took his outstretched hand. What more could I do? My jaw ached, but he was right and I knew it. I forgave him the blow. These days even the meekest, most docile men fell into a rage with less provocation.

"Tomorrow we work on casting," my master said, giving my shoulder a pat.

⁓⦿⁓

I owed Maestro Orazio another debt, but I didn't reveal it to him. That entire month under his tutelage I reverted to my old ways. I plotted; I stole. With each ring I engraved on his orders, tiny gold shavings dropped onto the floor. I picked them up and put them into the compartment of Nonna's poison ring. I hoarded them, waiting for just this moment, the moment I could take my hoard and create something bigger and more valuable.

One day, when my master and mistress were at mass, I took out Nonna's ring and poured gold shavings into a cast. I hammered it into a new solid unalloyed gold ring, shiny and complete, then to make it that much more attractive, I etched it with wildflowers. Those I took great care over, calling upon my memory of a hillside in Fiesole.

I waited for my moment, and then I crossed the street. I wore an apron over my tunic and a brown *mazzochio* on top of my head. My hair was still short, but I took no chances. I held a moldy cabbage in one hand. With the other, I fingered the ring in my apron pouch. It was still warm from the forges.

Now was the test. How good was my disguise? I'd been outside once before to aid Mamma, but this was different. That day I held people at a distance; today they would see me up close.

"Excuse me, *signor*," I asked the guard who wore the most garish uniform. He was a short man shaped like a butternut squash: long but round about the bottom. "I would like to see the traitorous Pazzi."

He looked me up and down, his eyes lingering on the smudges. Then he brought his sleeve up to his mouth and coughed. Even away from the forges I smelled like smoke.

"And who might you be?" he asked.

"Emilio, sir," I said. "The goldsmith's apprentice."

"What business have you with that villain?" he asked.

I showed him the cabbage. "He lives, that is my business. His every breath is an outrage. I want to show him that some of us do not forget."

I counted my heartbeats until he answered. One. Two. Three. Four.

"Boy," he said finally, "if I let in every citizen with a rotten cabbage the prison would smell worse than it already does and no one would be any richer." And he turned away from me.

I felt my heart drop in my chest. It didn't work. Then, God forgive me, I actually almost went back to the goldsmith's. I even took two paces back across the street. Then I fancied I heard Nonna's voice whispering in my ear: *coraggio.* Be brave. I realized Nonna would not give up so easily. Only a nitwit like Domenica would. I went back to the guard.

"I believe you dropped this," I said to his back, and I produced the golden ring.

He didn't look at my face, but he scrutinized the object in my hand. "Well, well," he said, taking it and putting it in a leather pouch that was strapped to his belt. "Emilio the goldsmith's apprentice. *Fratello mio.* Welcome to the Bargello."

He clapped me on the back and ushered me inside.

We walked through a passage to an open courtyard, where a horrible stench greeted my nostrils. I thought I was immune to stink because of my time in the forges, but the scent here was one hundred times worse than smoke. It was blood and feces and something even more awful.

In the middle of the courtyard was a bench made of stone, surrounded by a shallow moat of red water. Flies buzzed around it in one black cloud as we walked past. I fancied I saw bits of flesh and bone still stuck to its surface.

"What happened here?" I asked the guard.

He smiled a cruel smile and shrugged. "This and that. On Sundays the public gathers here to watch us mete out punishment to the wicked. Are you so tender that you have never been?"

"My master is harsh," I lied. "He makes me work Sundays."

"Console yourself," the jailer said, pointing to the slab. "Treason is a harsher master."

With that, my new *fratello* led me through a door and up a flight of stairs. On the second flight I wished I had a handkerchief to tie around my face. The stench inside was even worse than in the courtyard and soon I understood why. The prisoners — and there were more than I could count — were kept in cages smaller than they were. They could not stand up; they could not walk. The floors of some cages had a few bits of dirty straw, but most were just covered in excrement.

And the men inside those cages — *Madonna*! Most of them had untreated wounds leaking pus, great gaping holes where their eyes or ears or nose had been. As we walked past they crawled to the bars and reached out for us. "*Piacere, signori* . . . have mercy. I am an innocent man."

Those who had no tongues or no strength merely reached and uttered piteous moans. *Dream deep,* I willed them. *It's your only way out.*

Before I came in I thought this place was a slaughterhouse. Now I realized it was worse than a slaughterhouse. I wouldn't even treat livestock like this.

"Welcome to our *piano nobile,* fine enough to rival even the Pazzi *palazzo,*" the jailer smirked. He jabbed at the prisoners with his sword until they retreated back into heaps in the far corners of their cages. He didn't seem to need a handkerchief.

In the far corner we came to a cell large enough for a man to stand straight, even walk two paces across the length of it. There was a cot there as well. Atop the cot was a bundle of dirty, smelly rags, perhaps waiting for the laundry? That couldn't be. Clearly no washerwoman ever entered the Bargello.

The jailer banged on the bars. "Arise, worm! There is someone here to visit you."

As I watched, the rags stirred, revealing a gray face that was so gaunt it looked like a skull. The hair on the prisoner's head was thin and grew in clumps away from the oozing, festering sores, as though someone had dealt him blows but not enough to dent his skull, just enough to make him bleed and suffer. I didn't shriek. But in not shrieking, I bit my lips until they bled. Andrea. My real *fratello.*

"You might need to shred that before you throw it," the jailer said, indicating the cabbage I held in my left hand. "I'll be back to collect you in a few minutes. Enjoy yourself." Then he strolled off, as though he were walking through a meadow on a fine spring day.

"*Cretino,*" I muttered.

Over in his corner, Andrea sat crouched on his pallet. He stared at me without recognition. "Come to sport with the Pazzi vermin, eh? Let's get it over with."

I shook my head. I wanted to utter some words of comfort but was afraid. I was not eager to share information with Andrea's neighbors, much as I pitied them. "Come closer, Signor Pazzi, I would have a word with you," I said in my lowest, steadiest voice.

He snorted. "Where is the sport in that? No, *signor.* We must test your aim."

"What I have to say is for your ears alone," I said.

Andrea snorted. "When have I heard that before?"

I exhaled. "*Bene,*" I said. "I will speak from here. You may not remember me, but I used to labor in your father's palace. My name is Emilio. I was a friend to your sister. . . ."

Andrea sprang up and bolted to the cage. "Quiet, you idiot!" I had thought his rags would fall off him, he jumped so suddenly, but he was careful to keep his arms covered shoulder to fingertips. He was concealing something. His hands must have been bound before him in some manner, like Mamma's.

His eyes darted to the cages across the hall from him. "What news have you of my family?" he said in a whisper.

Seeing his face up close, feeling his fetid breath on my cheek, I thought: I have to get him out of here. I have to get him to Nonna. She'll fix him.

But there was no kitchen; no Nonna anymore. There was no one but me.

"Your father and brothers are dead, all save Antonio and Lionardo."

"This I knew," he said. "But what of my mother and sisters?"

"Your mother is exiled to Naples. Your sister Domenica is safe. She is sheltered at Our Lady of Fiesole."

"And Flora? What of Flora? Is she there as well?"

I shook my head. "Your sister would not remain in a convent. She is abroad," I whispered. My eyes darted to the left and right.

"And is she out of the reach of the Medici?"

"No one is out of the reach of the Medici," I said. "Not even God."

"Do not play with me so," Andrea said, and there were tears in his eyes. "Just tell me direct: is she safe?"

As he said this, he reached up to grip the bars of his prison. As he did so, the rags fell from his arms and I saw the truth of his fate.

The left hand was whole but grimy. But where his right hand used to be was just a stump. They had left a bony knot of a wrist, perhaps to remind him of what he'd lost. All that remained of the hand was coarse black thread sewn into a stump of putrid flesh.

"Your hand," I said, stifling an even larger shriek. "What happened to your hand?"

He put it behind his back. "I was to be drawn and quartered like my brothers but Father Alberto intervened. He vouched for my character and said I could have had nothing to do with the assassination. Instead I was found guilty of thievery."

"But how? You're no thief, Signor Andrea."

Andrea sighed wearily. "My father was found to be corrupt in all his business dealings. The ledgers were all in my hand. That alone made me guilty of thievery. You know the sentence for thievery."

Now I did. I had seen a bench earlier in the courtyard where the penalty had been carried out.

"I remember you now," Andrea said, searching my face. "You are that thin boy from Fiesole. You loved my sister. I marked it often."

"Then you were more observant than she was," I said.

Andrea sighed. "Go to her," he said. "Take her far away. I fear she is too close."

"Closer than you think," I said.

"Venice. She wanted to see Venice. Take her there."

"Your sister is stubborn," I said. "She has no teeth for adventure anymore."

"It's because of me, isn't it?" he said.

I had no answer for him. All I could do was shrug.

"Then we need to hatch a plot, you and I. You must tell her that you've seen me and that I'm already dead. That will set her free."

"No!" I said a little too loudly. "She will wonder why you don't hang with your brothers outside."

"I don't know. Tell her anything. Tell her that I was to be dumped in the Arno. Please, I don't care what you tell her. Just get her out of the city. And quickly."

I gathered myself. "No. I will not lie for you. But I will tell her this: that you promised me you will try to stay alive if she leaves. And I must have your word that it will be so. You must see, Signor Andrea, that you are the only family she has left."

"Our mother and sisters still breathe," he said.

"Do I need to say it?" I told him through gritted teeth. "You are the only one who matters. To her, that is."

I saw my brother's eyes well up. "I thought . . . ," he began, then stopped and shook his head. "What you ask isn't easy. To survive this ordeal I've been telling myself that I'm made of stone. Stone can't feel."

I shook my head. "Not stone," I said. "Gold. Gold can be melted and broken and even tortured . . ." I forced myself to say that last word, even though I knew that by saying it I gave the word power. "But it always keeps its value."

The moaning of the prisoners on the far end of the hall grew louder. The jailer was coming back.

Andrea looked to the end of the hall. He reached his good hand through the bars and clasped my fingers. "*Bene.* We have a deal," he said in a rush. "Mind you, hold her dear. Just take her away. Venice, Rome, Naples . . . perhaps Milan. Frederico Barbarossa has no love for the Medici."

"I will hold you to your promise," I said. "You will stay alive."

"And I to yours," he said. "Now throw it." He retreated into a crouch in the corner of his cell.

I had forgotten about the cabbage. "Throw it!" he repeated, this time more forcefully.

I did as he said. "And may you burn in hell," I spat. The cabbage impacted on the wall behind him and shreds of it landed on his clumpy hair. He said nothing, nor did he wipe it away. He had already reverted to his molten state.

I turned around and pretended I hadn't seen the jailer coming. "You," Signor Butternut said, motioning to me and smiling in a way I didn't like. "The sheriff wants a word."

Chapter Twenty-one

I was ushered to a small room on the fourth floor of the prison, the Arno side. My jailer friend showed me in.

"Here's the boy you wanted, Signor Valentini," he said, and closed the door behind him. As soon as the door was shut, the screams of the prisoners became muffled. Signor Valentini? The monster who persecuted children for not eating their mush?

A man in an elaborate brocade tunic was standing behind a desk. On his desk was a marble bust of Dante. I recognized it as one of the objects from our old Madonna gallery.

Signor Valentini stood with his back to me, staring out a

window to the hills beyond the river. He had a lovely view. From here it almost seemed a reasonable room of a reasonable man in a gentle town of reasonable people.

"I never forget a face, you know," he said, still with his back turned. With his words, it felt as though he hacked off all my bravery until it fell in shards about my feet. I balled my hands to fists at my sides to still the shaking.

He turned around. *Madonna!* I knew this man. He no longer wore the simple tunic of the Medici guard, but it was the same man from our *palazzo* — the one who read the proclamation, beheaded Captain Umberto, and ordered my father drawn and quartered. He hunted and tortured and killed us. He was my enemy.

"You're the goldsmith's apprentice," he said. "I see you through the window bent over a workbench. Tell me: what business have you with the last living Pazzi?"

"Curiosity," I muttered, willing my voice as low as it could go. I was amazed I could even utter words.

"Indeed?" he said, and produced from behind his back the gold ring I'd slipped to the jailer out front. He leaned across his desk. "This is a lavish bribe for someone only satisfying idle curiosity. A joint of beef would have served just as well."

This must be how it started for all the others, I thought. Brought in here, asked an insinuating question by a narrow man with a piercing glare.

In the face of such a glare, I decided the best lie was the one that contained the most truth.

"I knew Signor Andrea. I was once a worker in the Pazzi *palazzo*. A member of the guard."

"Ah . . . ," the sheriff said, savoring my statement as though it were some delicate wine. "A Pazzi sympathizer. I should have known."

"Not entirely," I said. "I had little love for most of them. Signor Jacopo was a greedy, conniving man, and most of the sons were no better. And compared to Signora Maddelena those cretins were all modesty and virtue."

The sheriff waved me off. "Empty words from a boy trying to save his own skin," he said. "Nothing I haven't heard a thousand times before."

"But," I continued, "Signor Andrea was cut from a different cloth than the rest. He studied at Pisa. He valued reason above money. He is an honest man, sir."

The sheriff walked around his desk, stroking his chin with his hand. Not once did he look me in the face.

"Listen, he needs help. The flesh around his arm is diseased. It needs to be treated or else he will die."

I said the last part quickly before I lost my nerve.

"*Basta*," the sheriff said. "I am uninterested in righteousness. I am more interested in guilt. Now I want to know: does your current master know you use his gold for jailer's bribes?"

I forced myself to breathe. He had me. He knew it; I knew it.

"No, *signore*. He knows nothing about this."

"But the gold. It is yours? He gave it to you freely?"

"No, *signore.*"

"Then you took it?"

"*Si, signore.* I picked up little flecks of gold from the floor. The leftovers from engraving. He didn't miss them."

"Whether he misses them or not the fact is you took them without asking. Do you know what that makes you?"

My throat was dry; I swallowed hard. "It makes me a thief, *signore.*"

The sheriff looked me in the eye. I looked back.

"*Bene.* So we are clear on that point. You are a thief and a conspirator. By all rights you deserve to die. *Il Magnifico* himself has declared it: this town has been infested with Pazzi. We must purge ourselves of them and anyone who knew them lest we ourselves become tainted."

Slowly, he walked around me, inspecting me.

"Let me share something with you," he said, stopping by my left ear. "I was there," he whispered, an uncomfortable buzz.

I know; I saw you at the *palazzo,* I wanted to say. But I held my tongue and tried not to stare at the blade strapped to his belt.

That wasn't what he was talking about, anyway. "Easter morning at the *duomo,* when the assassins killed Giuliano," he said. "As I mentioned before: I never forget a face. So I know something *Il Magnifico* doesn't like to remember. A Pazzi saved his life."

As he said those words I began to remember, a lean face urging me toward the sacristy. *This way, signorina . . .*

"It was a Pazzi daughter, no older than you are. She rushed forward to save *Il Magnifico* when the whole town, myself included, stood still as a statue from shock and confusion.

"At first I thought she was the daughter we'd all heard about, the renowned beauty. But then her veil came off and I saw it was a different daughter. The one who helped her nonna tend to the sick. Her name was Lorenza. Everyone knew her as . . ." He sniffed the air, as though he could divine my name through his nose.

"Flora," I finished for him.

"Flora. Just so. She had a boy with her. That one was no coward, either. I saw him slit the neck of one of the assassins from ear to ear. The two of them acted with great bravery. Without them my master's life would have been forfeit as well as his brother's. Such courage is not easily forgotten. So you see, you can't fool me. I remember you, Emilio."

And with that, even though nothing in the room had changed, I felt him release me.

He walked back to his desk, tossing my ring up and down, up and down. "You realize, of course, that I must pretend that all Pazzi and everyone who ever knew the Pazzi are vipers. So if you come back inside the prison I will be forced to arrest you. You do not want that."

He tried my ring on one crooked finger, then another, until he found one that fit.

"This is a fine piece of craftsmanship. Done by your own hand, you say?"

I nodded.

"Young talent should be encouraged. If you were to send more such pieces, with or without your master's blessing, I might be persuaded to have Signor Andrea's wounds seen to. I might even be persuaded to make his life tolerable. But know this: *tolerable* is all I can manage. *Il Magnifico* will never pardon him. He will die here, never again seeing the outside of his cell. I tell you this so you will not entertain false hope."

I nodded. "May I leave now?"

He motioned me out. "As long as we understand each other."

I opened the door, letting in a blast of torment like heat from a forge.

"Emilio," the sheriff called. I turned around. He came back to me, stood in front of my face so close I could see the fine wrinkles like tiny brooms gathered around his eyes, and the tufts of dark hair growing in his nostrils. He shot me a soft look — one that was not narrow and mean. Then he reached up a hand and caressed my cheek with calloused fingers. I did not flinch.

"If you see Signorina Flora, tell her to stay hidden. She had a kind face. I would like to see it remain on her neck."

◦◦◦

When my master and his wife came back from mass that afternoon they found me hunched over my workbench as though nothing unusual had happened. Signora Maria sniffed the air around me distastefully. "Time for a bath, Emilio. It's been over a month. Fetch some water from the well and I'll put the tub out."

"Is that wise, Maria? Sending her out like that?" Orazio asked.

I convinced them that it would be fine for me to go to the well if I wore a kerchief over my nose. As indeed I did.

It took at least twelve trips to the well to fetch sufficient water to fill the tub. It should have taken me six, but I shook so hard I spilled half. Along the way I tried to puzzle through how much the sheriff knew, whether he thought me Emilio or Flora. *I never forget a face,* he'd said. And the expression in his eyes when he'd caressed my cheek at the end of the interview — it was tender, the closest I would ever come to a lover's embrace. Did he truly know me or not? In the end I decided it didn't matter. Caught was caught. I had been disguised as a boy so my nose was forfeit. I had been stealing so my right hand was forfeit. I had been born a Pazzi so my head was forfeit. I lived only because of his grace. That was the message he'd wanted to send. Every bone in my body told me I needed to leave town and leave now.

And yet I stayed as weeks turned to seasons and seasons turned to years. I spent my time hunched over a workbench, little marking the world outside other than to know that my Andrea never swung from the prison walls. I collected metal shavings from the floor. I crafted things — rings, crosses, salt shakers, and small blades: daggers and *squarcatos*. And every fourth Sunday while my master and mistress were at mass, I crossed the street and delivered my trinkets to the squash-shaped guard who stood in front of the Bargello. Signor Butternut I still called him, but never to his face.

I tried to be quiet about it every time; every time he greeted me expansively. "Emilio! *Fratello mio!*" he would call, and kiss me sloppily on the cheek.

"How fares the prisoner?" I would whisper.

"Not so good," he said. "You know how things are." At first his answer startled me into believing that Andrea was worse than I had last seen. But Signor Butternut answered the same each time, and I began to understand that *not so good* meant *not dead,* and that Andrea had held to his promise to stay alive.

Slowly, I began to think of my brother less. That is to say, not every instant of every day. And my mind turned to other things. Memories crowded in. And with them, Nonna's voice, saying I had left something undone. But what? I asked myself. Mamma was safe; Domenica was safe. Andrea was alive; the rest were dead. Even Emilio, wielding his wheel of cheese. Dead through my lie.

Then finally, on Easter morning I remembered another Easter a full year before, and cradling a man's head as his life bled out of him onto steps of an altar, and I remembered my promise.

My first gift to Giuliano's son was a little silver spoon. Into the handle I cast a frolicking puppy, something to make a small boy laugh. When I was done, I stole away to the confessionals at the *duomo,* waited for the one with Father Alberto to empty, and knelt within.

"In the name of the Father, Son, and Holy Ghost," he said. I couldn't see his face behind the grille.

"Bless me, Father, for I have sinned. I have killed at least three men; two with a knife; one with a lie. I disrespected my father and mother. I hated my sister. I spat in the soup."

There was silence on the other side. "Do you repent any of this?"

"Yes," I said. "I repent it all." He was about to speak but I didn't let him. If I didn't finish this task then I never would. "I have brought an object with me. I desire you to deliver this to the ironmonger's shop by Fort Belvedere. The ironmonger has a daughter named Carolina. This is a present for her son."

Then I fled again, not waiting for my penance.

When I was outside I pulled a dirty kerchief over my face as I did whenever I went out. I did this partly so that no one would recognize me, partly a self-imposed penance for my role in that terrible day the year before. I was no innocent to be frolicking in any Eden. So I deprived myself of fresh air. It was a small penance but I convinced myself that God took note.

Two days later we awoke before dawn to a banging on our door.

I sprinted up from my pallet. "I'll get it," I muttered to my master and mistress, and fumbled for a candle to light my way.

"Wait, Emilio," Orazio called after me. "It's not safe!"

The banging continued downstairs. I pulled a *mazzochio* over my head and unbarred the door. Signor Valentini came in. Alone. He slammed the door behind him.

"You," he said, pointing a finger at me, "are a very foolish young man."

His voice and face were hard.

"What's going on down here?" My master came down the stairs hastily, only half-dressed. He saw the face of our guest and nearly tripped over his feet. He recovered himself as best he could. "Signor Valentini. Welcome. What brings you to our humble shop?"

"This," Signor Valentini said. With a gloved hand he reached into the purse attached to his belt and pulled out the silver spoon. "Is this your work?"

My master examined the spoon, the form and the engravings, then shot me a thunderous look. "No, indeed, *signor*. There is no stamp. I stamp all my work. A point of honor."

"Pity," he said, sitting down on a bench by the window, putting his dirty boots up on a table. "I have been charged by my mistress with finding its maker."

"Your mistress?"

"Signora Lucrezia de Medici. Mistress to us all. This was a gift to her poor overlooked grandson, Giulianino, the natural son of Giuliano de Medici."

"Was it indeed," my master said, and I took a step back, trying to seem part of the woodwork.

"Signora de Medici is a shrewd woman," Signor Valentini said, placing special emphasis on the word *shrewd,* as though it were an insult. "But she loves her children. She will never get over the death of her poor, murdered son."

"I understand, Signor Valentini. I too know what it is to have lost a child."

"*Allora.* Then you will know that Giulianino is her only comfort, and why she was pleased to find someone else had not forgotten him."

Maestro Orazio stroked his beard. "Pleased?" he repeated.

"Deeply," said Signor Valentini, and he took from his belt a purse of coins and threw it at him.

With great difficulty, my master tore his eyes away from the purse and examined the spoon I'd made. "May I take this item with me to the next goldsmith's meeting? Perhaps someone there will know."

"*Bene,*" Signor Valentini said. "Tell them there are more florins for the artist if more baubles could be made. One more thing: perhaps it is best for us all if the artist does not step forward. Tell him to use Father Alberto. Whatever you do, do not send the lackwit who opened the door." He pointed to me.

"Emilio?" my master said, cuffing me on the head. "He will make a fine craftsman one day, sir. But I fear he lacks common sense."

"See you drill it into him, sir. These are bleak times, Orazio. I have been a busy man."

"Well have we marked it," my master said blandly.

"Then you will also have marked that I perform my duties with relish. But persecuting innocents? I don't bother with that if I can help it. There is no sport to it."

"I'm sure you are a just man, Signor Valentini. I shall do as you bid."

As soon as he left Maestro Orazio dealt me a blow that set my right eye spinning in my socket. The flesh around it swelled up and by midmorning it looked like an eggplant. Then he picked me up off the floor and bade me confess all. I told him about everything — the little shavings I'd picked up after engraving, my visit to the Bargello, my bribes to Signor Valentini, my drop-off at Father Alberto's confessional. When I was done I could see he wanted to kill me with his bare hands, and would have but for the purse of coins jangling on the tabletop. That much I knew to be true: I was becoming an accomplished craftsman. He needed money; therefore, he needed me. And the blow? It wasn't repeated; my eye healed. I began to understand later that he hit me in the one particular place Signor Valentini was likely to see from across the street.

That day he just picked up the purse and walked away. "I swear, Emilio," he said. "You'll be the death of me."

I couldn't deny it. Not with my history.

Chapter Twenty-two

Florence, 1482

It has now been almost a week since Signor Botticelli came to the shop.

After he left, I asked Maestro Orazio to bring me a quill and a bit of paper. He looked at me as though I asked for the moon, but produced them all the same. I have been writing this on the backs of his old accounts.

For the past week I've been pulling these images, sharp and painful, from the forges of memory. I've spared myself nothing. There are a few details that remain to end my narrative, and I'm determined to do so by tomorrow when I deliver Botticelli's commission. My time is near, I can feel it like a change in the wind.

What more to say about four years of hard work? I labored, I ate, I slept. And gradually I forgot everything but my own guilt. It was clear I had a hand in my family's tragedy. Had I not helped save Lorenzo de Medici, my father's scheme might have turned out differently. But working here with gold makes me remember a jeweled hand, reaching out from under a sea of black robes. No matter how I might wish to have behaved otherwise, I know I could never have stood by watching those fingers curl and relax for even an instant more than I did.

I have been slowly losing the texture of my former life. The sight of my brothers swinging from the Bargello walls — after a while they just became things to me. Straw men shedding their stuffing in the wind. Andrea's tormented face when I last saw him? It is just a shape, a pair of sunken cheekbones. I remember Papa's red cap but not the head underneath; I remember Domenica's hair, but she no longer turns around to face me. Even of Nonna all that remains is one gray braid sweeping her crooked back.

But there is one I don't forget, nor will I, no matter how long I live. It is for his sake that I draw out these memories, even the painful ones, beginning with the day the messenger of the gods came to my *palazzo* and vomited in our oranges.

I remember Emilio's brown curly hair and the gap in his front teeth. I remember that he was skinny and ill, then he was not. I remember how I felt when he smiled. I remember the night we stood together in the kitchen, watching

Domenica and Captain Umberto whisper to each other in the firelight. *Amore per sempre.* I remember him saying, "Thank God we'll never be like that." I was confused at the time, thinking he meant *we* — Emilio and I — would never be in love. Now I realize he wasn't saying that at all: he was saying we were too smart to make promises we couldn't keep.

Then I remember all the things Emilio did during our short time together. Like the time he attacked a man twice his size just for pushing me, or him leaning out the kitchen window, brandishing a wheel of cheese, waving off Signor Botticelli. *Not that one, eh? I need that one.* I remember reaching for his hand when I wanted to help him or just be with him, and how, even though those moments weren't ornate or even pretty, they nourished me more than the finest art.

Finally, I remember him standing on a hilltop, not meeting my eyes. *I don't love the others,* he had said, in a voice so soft and low I thought it was the wind.

You were wrong about me, Emilio. I did turn out like Domenica. I made you an empty promise. I want to tell you I didn't understand then because I had only the illusion to guide me. I hated the pretty words that passed between lovers but I wanted to hear them spoken. And now that I am like Signor Botticelli and able to see the true beauty in my life, it's too late. You're gone.

This is what keeps me here in this hell so terrible I think it must have been dreamt by Father Alberto. *This* is what I will never stop atoning for, no matter how many spoons

Giuliano's son delights in, how many rings adorn the sheriff's fingers. *This* is why Signor Botticelli's visit has transformed me from hard metal back into some whining, pampered nitwit.

I grow tired of baubles.

I want to go home.

Chapter Twenty-three

This morning, after a night of thrashing sleeplessly, I shoo my master and mistress to high mass. "Are you sure, Flora?" Maria says. "Perhaps Orazio should accompany you. Signor Botticelli said nothing about your coming alone."

I tell her it is all right, that she and her husband had already done enough.

She caresses my face. *"Carissima,"* she says. "You stopped being a debt a long time ago. If you want us to, we will come."

"I thought you didn't want any more family," I say.

Signora Maria tears up and rushes from the room.

"I can see that our influence hasn't improved your manners," Orazio says. "That was a fine parting."

I call Maria back and apologize. I tell her I will be fine and send them on their way.

Am I sad that my time is at an end? Not really. It's time I took my place alongside my brothers as I should have four years ago.

There is a tub of bathwater upstairs in the apartment. Both Signora Maria and Maestro Orazio have already used it so the water is not clean, but it is clean enough. I unwrap the hair I haven't seen in four years. It falls to my waist. I wash myself as best I can, but when I get out of the tub I still smell like a volcano. I put on Maria's second dress and remember days when I thought dresses shabby because they lacked pearls.

Outside, I turn my uncovered face to the sun. The air isn't exactly fresh — it smells of horse poop and turgid water from the Arno — but I breathe it as though a fine perfume. I'm not really breaking my bargain with God, I reason. This is my death march. Surely a doomed person deserves to breathe open air?

My first act is to cross the street. "Signor Butternut!" I call loudly and wave. I kiss him sloppily on the cheek. "*Buongiorno,* fratello mio! Is this not a glorious day? I have to go now, but I shall most likely be back in a moment. *Ciao!*"

And I leave him to stare after me like some dumb beast.

I make my progress up the Via dei Balastrieri, my head held high, my skirts held up but only high enough that they don't drag in the muck. It is a fine spring day. People stare as I walk past — men especially. I imagine what they're thinking. *Murderer. Traitor.*

I find Signor Botticelli's address and knock on the back door.

A maid answers, a squat woman with a harelip. At first glance she is not beautiful, yet I know she must be, else Signor Botticelli would not employ her. She looks me up and down. "This will not do. This will not do at all," she says.

She pulls me inside and pours me a new bath, this time with clean hot water. She takes a brush to my hair and face and begins to scrub. She is not gentle. "Leave me alone," I tell her. "I know how to bathe."

"No, you don't," she says, whacking me on the head with a brush. "You're filthy. Now sit still."

But I don't want to sit still. I don't want to watch as she scrubs away everything I've so carefully built up. I don't want to see what's underneath.

The black is the first layer to go. Then the red.

When she is satisfied that I am clean, she produces a linen towel. "Dry yourself," she says. "Then Maestro Alessandro says that you are to put this on and join him upstairs in his studio. He is expecting you."

She hangs a gown from a beam in the ceiling as if it were a bunch of sage. When she is gone, I step out of the tub and examine the dress. The material is soft and light — almost transparent. Embroidered all over are tiny flowers in pink and green and yellow. Even Domenica would not turn up her nose at such a fine vestment.

What is Signor Botticelli up to? Why bring me here at all,

dress me like this? Perhaps this is Signora de Medici's desire, that I have one last reminder of something fine before she exacts my punishment. Very well, then. She has asked for a Pazzi; a Pazzi she shall have.

I take the ring I made for Signora de Medici, mount the stairs, and throw open the door the maid indicated to me.

Inside is a space as large as our great hall used to be — an open room with wooden floors and huge leaded windows facing south. I do not see Signora de Medici, but Signor Botticelli is there, standing with his back to me, inspecting a draped canvas as tall as he is and twice as long.

Around him a dozen aproned apprentices busy themselves grinding and mixing. One of them, carrying a paint jar, sees me enter.

"Madonna!" he says as his mouth drops along with the paint. Blue splatters all over the wooden floor.

The rest turn around and stare just as long. "I didn't believe it," mutters another apprentice. "You told us but I didn't believe it."

Signor Botticelli himself turns around and looks as well. He is wearing a face I've never seen before. He is neither the upstairs toady nor the downstairs dishwasher I remember. His expression is serious. Maybe, I think, this is his *true* face; his working face.

He wipes his hands on a paint-splattered smock and comes up to me. Up close I can see how he's aged in four years. His sandy hair is mostly gray; his heft now makes him look tired instead of prosperous. His eyes and chins sag like heavy purses.

He twists a lock of my hair over my shoulder and pinches a fleck of dust from my sleeve. "Very well," he says to his apprentices. "I promised you all one look. When you are done gawking you may leave us. And one of you fetch us some wine. I am in a festive mood."

One by one they set down their tools and file past me. None looks away from my face until they are gone.

Signor Botticelli closes the door on the nose of the last one, and examines my hands. "I don't need to ask where you've been all these years," he says, pointing to a scar on my palm. "How could you let this happen to you?"

"*Basta,*" I say, and slap him away. "Quit fussing with me. Where is your patroness?"

Signor Botticelli seems perplexed. "This is not what I expected, but I forget you have reason to be suspicious. Very well. I thought we could go straight to overindulging, but I see we must get the unpleasantness out of the way first."

I look over his shoulder and out the window. How many horses are below? Is there one for each of my limbs?

"You've been pardoned," Signor Botticelli says. "Signora Lucrezia de Medici has deemed you no longer a threat to her or her kin. You are free. You cannot remain in Florence, but you have her word that you will not be pursued."

It is my turn to gawk.

"Close your mouth, Flora. It's an unbecoming expression."

"I've been pardoned? For what?"

"For being a traitor, I suppose. It's too dangerous for you to remain any longer, Flora. You've changed in four years. Everyone can see that. Signor Valentini himself has been whispering about the apprentice in Maestro Orazio's shop who looks nothing like a boy but a lot like a Pazzi. Everyone has. One of these days someone will inform *Il Magnifico*."

I purse my lips. "I saved his life," I say.

"So Father Alberto tells me. *Il Magnifico* has chosen to forget that fact, Flora, as should you. If you remind him he will silence you and quickly. He does not like to be thought of as a weak man, still breathing by the grace of a fragile young maid."

"Hardly fragile," I mutter. "And definitely not young. Not anymore."

He smiles with half of his mouth, then turns around and rummages through a cupboard. "I wouldn't say that, Flora. You're not old. Just different. Most people experience the spring of their lives first. But you, *cara mia,* jumped straight into winter."

I don't know what he's talking about, my life in winter. For the past four years my life has had only one season: hot.

He is still rummaging through his cupboard. "Never fear, though, Flora. By my expert planning I have ensured that it will not be winter forever. Now where did that woman put that thing? Here it is! Still fresh." When he emerges he carries a wreath woven with real wildflowers, which he lays upon my head. I don't have a chance to bury my nose in them. But I don't have to. Their smell floats down from my hair, a fresh and subtle scent, and I feel something inside me crack.

Signor Botticelli stands back. Can he really be oblivious to the pain this crown causes me? He sensed heartbreak in Domenica, for God's sake. And yet he seems not to notice my distress.

He continues: "A year after the April Rebellion, Father Alberto came to me with a strange tale of a youth in a confessional with a low but familiar voice who admitted to things — he didn't tell me which things — he knew you had done. He said that at first he tried to chase you but you were too quick. But you came back, each time with a bauble for the son of the unfortunate Giuliano. He followed you in secret to Maestro Orazio's.

"He was not certain about your identity and had the excellent sense to consult with me. He knew I'd painted in your *palazzo* before that terrible day and thought I might be *simpatico.*"

Well, are you? I wanted to say. *I've never been able to figure that out.*

Instead I let him finish his tale.

"By then I had already heard rumors from other sources about an apprentice in my old goldsmith shop. A youth with a dirty face but even the dirt could not hide his disturbing beauty. So after Father Alberto's visit I sent my first apprentice to observe you. He came back with this sketch."

Signor Botticelli produces a notebook from atop a marble pedestal and opens it to the first page. There I am in black and white, sitting in front of an anvil, my head in a wrap. I turn the page. There I am in profile. Here is page after page of details about me in this notebook, my hands, my arms, the curve of my neck. *Madonna!* My every move has been scrutinized.

"I stood outside Orazio's too and saw for myself. I had no doubts. I still recognized the girl who crashed into me in her grandmother's garden — the one chased by the wind."

"So I've been pardoned," I say. "But why now? You say I've changed and I'm no longer safe. I say the change is not exactly new. Why do I have to be pardoned at this very moment?"

"Because only now, with Count Riorio dead, did Signora de Medici give me her blessing."

"And you would never do anything without it," I spit.

Signor Botticelli shrugs. "Would you?"

I think of the horses that pulled my father apart. Nothing justified that. No, I will never again do anything against Medici wishes.

"I am what I am, Flora. My fortunes depend on others. But, occasionally, I do get to behave in the manner I like. Today for example. I don't mind telling you that Father Alberto and I have hatched a plot that even puts your father to shame. The second part of our scheme should be arriving shortly. The first I am pleased to show you now. You, my dear, are the first to see my *Primavera*."

He stands by the covered canvas, and there is a glint in his eye I recognize from old. He is very pleased with himself. "You're *really* going to thank me for this one," he says.

With that, he throws back the drapery.

This is no Madonna. It is a garden scene — several figures are celebrating in an orchard with trees with round fruit — fruit that looks like the *palle* of the Medici — and soft cushiony grass underneath.

I look at two figures in particular.

On the far left is a handsome brown-haired youth with wings on his sandals. He reaches up and stirs clouds with his sword. I reach out and stroke his painted brown curls and I remember a different boy, riding so fast down from the hills it looked as though he was flying. "The messenger of the gods," I mutter.

"Recognize that one, do you?"

I nod and take my fingers off the canvas. "Mercury."

Right of center in the front is a fair-haired goddess in a white, almost transparent gown embroidered with flowers, and a wreath upon her hair — a bit like my garb today. She holds delicate blossoms in the fold of her dress, about to scatter them.

I recognize the face at once.

"Beautiful," I say. "You have captured Domenica perfectly."

"Domenica? You think that is she? No, my dear. You are mistaken." He points to the woman behind, a sad Venus in a heavy red cloak. "This is Domenica back there. This is her realm but not her story."

"If that's Domenica, then who's this?" I point to the goddess in front, the graceful one.

"Who do you think it is, *Flora*?"

I start to shake then. I shake and I can't stop. It's as if inside me there is a catastrophe going on, the kind that swallows houses and brings caves of ice crashing down from mountaintops.

I look to the two remaining figures, the ones on the far right of the canvas, and I know.

These last two are a man and a woman. The man has a blue pallor and floats through the air. He blows on the woman but at the same time his arms are open as if to catch her.

The woman, another fair-haired beauty, runs from him in terror. Flowers spill from her mouth as if she is vomiting them. The blue-faced figure is Zephyrus, God of the West Wind, and the one running in terror is Chloris, the girl I was until today.

I look away from the canvas from the woman in the white dress, the goddess with the flowers. I'm still uncertain. Two faces? Both mine?

Signor Botticelli sees my confusion. "How long has it been since you've looked at your reflection?" he asks.

The last time was in the well in Fiesole, after I cut my hair and dirtied my face. "A while," I say aloud.

He produces a bit of polished glass the size of a human head from his cupboard. "Here. It isn't large. But it should be enough."

I take it from him and slowly raise it to my face. I am strong, I tell myself, and I have the scars on my hands to prove it. What can the mirror show me that can be worse than what I see through the shop window every day?

But it is worse. Much worse. I drop the mirror and it shatters on the floor. I bury my face in my hands and weep. It is no dainty weeping, either. I honk like a goose. I recovered from the slaughter of my own family, but I will never recover from the sight of my own face.

"I didn't know," I manage to say. "I never realized how much I look like Nonna."

Signor Botticelli hands me his kerchief and rests his hand on my shoulder. "You have her spirit, *signorina*. *That* is what you couldn't disguise. *That* is how I recognized you even though your face was smeared with ash. And that is what makes you so beautiful."

I look up at his canvas again. There is no mistaking the story now. Venus. Mercury. Zephyrus. Chloris. And finally, Flora, a goddess with a serene face — a woman who stood tall in her suffering.

There is a knock at the door. "*Avanti!*" Signor Botticelli

calls, and there's that glint in his eyes again. "I hope you don't mind. I've invited others to my unveiling."

Two men enter the studio. The first I recognize instantly. His tonsured hair is streaked with gray now, but he still wears a threadbare habit; the same wooden cross hangs from his neck.

"*Grazie a Dio,*" Father Alberto says as he comes toward me, his arms open wide. "I thought it was you. But I wasn't as certain as Signor Botticelli. I am so pleased to see you alive and well."

He embraces me then stands back. He clasps my hands and unclasps them, then embraces me again. "I thought you were lost to us."

The man with him I don't recognize at all. He is taller than I am — practically a giant. I'm sure if he stood on a mountain he could touch the sky. His shoulders are broad. He wears a tunic that is stretched tight across the muscles in his arms. His brown curly hair falls about his shoulders. And his face, *Madonna!* His features are so fine and so handsome to gaze upon, he makes Captain Umberto look like a toothless old hag.

The man stares at me just as Signor Botticelli's apprentices did. I blot my face with Botticelli's handkerchief and extend a hand to this stranger.

"I don't believe we've met, *signor,*" I say.

The man smiles at me. The smile begins in his brown eyes and spreads to his two crooked front teeth.

"Flora," he whispers, and gives my hand a familiar squeeze.

⤜⊚⤛

What I felt earlier that day when Signor Botticelli unveiled my painting, my *Primavera,* wasn't a catastrophe — it was merely a thaw.

Now, as Emilio smiles at me, I finally bloom.

Epilogue

Nonna was wrong. She said that what made Flora — the original Flora — change into a goddess was her suffering. Now, many years later, I know that while her suffering may have shaped her, it was her ability to forgive that made her divine.

First, she had to forgive the goddess Diana for slaughtering her family. She also had to forgive her own stupid mother Niobe for raining destruction down on them.

Last and most difficult, she had to forgive herself for surviving.

⤳✾⤶

"They call me Mercuzio now," Emilio said when he let me go at last, that day in Signor Botticelli's studio. He kept touching my face, my hair, the scars on my hands. I felt his fingers as though they were a balm. And his smile, *Madonna!* It wasn't the open smile from the scrawny boy who wielded wooden swords and wheels of cheese. It was a whispering smile — the kind I used to long for as I watched Domenica and Captain Umberto embrace in my garden.

I took his hands in my own and counted all the fingers. As I caressed his face I inventoried his features: one nose, two eyes, two ears. Then I bade him kiss me again. He possessed one tongue; all his teeth; sweet breath that smelled of ginger from the Orient.

Then Emilio admired my painting. I told him it wasn't *my* painting, and that, like everything else that passed through my hands, it was going to the Medici.

"A wedding present for a cousin, I believe," Signor Botticelli said. "But I wanted you two to see it first."

"Do they know you used a Pazzi as a model?" I asked him.

His face turned stormy. "No. Nor will they ever. I'm not like you, Flora. I value my own skin."

Emilio grasped my hand and told Signor Botticelli he didn't mind giving *Il Magnifico* the painting as long as he got to keep the real thing. And me? I was pleased as well, although I couldn't help thinking of Mamma. She didn't have a Pazzi-Medici wedding in real life, but a Pazzi would watch over a Medici bridal chamber, perhaps for all eternity. It was a small, secret victory, but I had grown to like secrets. Perhaps I was more of a Pazzi than I cared to admit.

The four of us drank wine from jeweled goblets. Signor Botticelli toasted himself. "To my genius!" he said with a raised glass. "I only hope I have done you two justice." Emilio and I told him that yes, he'd done us more than justice, that it was one of the best works of art we'd ever seen. Signor Botticelli drank in the praise more readily than the wine; I thought he would never get his fill.

But eventually he did, and I turned my attention once again to my flesh-and-blood Mercuzio.

"I thought you were dead," I said. "What happened to you?"

He looked away from the canvas and back to me. "I could ask the same," he said, but he didn't seem angry. "You weren't at the convent like we agreed. Your sister was there. She told me she'd seen you die."

"She said *what*?" That *bestia*. I can't believe there was ever a moment when I thought I might like her. She disposed of my future twice — first with my flawed diamonds, the second when she sent away my love.

"Dead dead dead. You. Dead," Emilio said. "She painted a convincing picture. She said she'd seen your head sliced clean off your body."

That detail made me remember Captain Umberto's last stand in my father's library. Had Domenica seen past me, past the fire in the hearth, to the battle? Or did she just make up that detail to convince Emilio? It made no difference. The result was the same.

"I waited for you for three days," Emilio said. "I slept outside the convent gate. I knew if you were alive you would come back. Finally I gave up and came back to Father Alberto, who gave me our purse and bid me ride to Rome to petition the pope to take action. Which he did finally with the excommunication."

"Too late for my brothers," I said. "Where was his army?"

Emilio shook his head sadly. "Still in Rome. Awaiting a Pazzi victory that didn't come."

"Coward," I muttered.

"Easy, Flora. You're talking about God's representative on earth," Father Alberto reminded me. "Him we may not question."

Emilio was still talking. "All those days, running here and there. Rome. Milan. Naples. Begging for soldiers; begging for mercy. Messenger of the gods, indeed. There were days I thought I would dissolve into a pool of lather like my horses. And to what end?"

"*Stupido,*" Signor Botticelli said, cuffing him on the head. Emilio ducked as though he were a rickety boy instead of a colossus of a man. Signor Botticelli had that effect on both of us. "That you might live to see today and marry your sweetheart and be happy."

Then he explained the rest of the Botticelli–Father Alberto

plot: Emilio and I marry here, then I accompany my new husband back to Milan, where Duke Frederico Barbarossa valued my swain's counsel so much, he deeded him a vast amount of land and so many purses of gold that Emilio practically needed a bank of his own to store it. Ah, well. I didn't mind his riches as long as they didn't turn him into my father. I counted us safe on that score.

"Of course it's up to you," Emilio said. "If you prefer I can take you to your vile sister at Our Lady of Fiesole. I will even take you to Venice and book you passage on a ship bound for the Holy Lands."

Did I love Emilio because he was so blessed with loveliness his eyes shone with it? Did I love him because we'd played and then suffered together? Or did I love him simply because I was so relieved to see him alive and whole that I wept another Arno on Signor Botticelli's floor? I'll never know. But I choose to believe that, just as Signor Botticelli saw my spirit, I saw his, and I knew he was the one person in the world with whom I could be free.

And that was why I held back. "I can't," I told him. "Andrea will die if I don't keep sending trinkets to Signor Valentini."

Emilio had an answer for that too. "I'm rich, remember," he said, and he smiled a goofy smile.

"Please, Emilio. This is no sporting matter. I'm talking about Andrea's life."

"*Carissima,* I love you, but I see the smoke has made you

dense. I meant to say: *I* can send the bribes to Signor Valentini for Andrea's upkeep."

Upkeep. As though he were some kind of pet. "What about his release?" I asked Signor Botticelli. "Will my brother be pardoned too?"

Signor Botticelli shook his head sadly. "I fear in this matter *Il Magnifico* cannot be acted upon."

Father Alberto patted me on the back. "Do not give up hope, Flora," he said gently. "Not while Andrea has friends and a sister such as yourself. That is very much in his favor."

"Think of it, *carissima*," Emilio said. "We could both labor on your brother's behalf. I could continue planting words in Barbarossa's ear about your brother's plight; or you could yourself. That might be better. He likes pretty girls *and* he likes tales of suffering. The two of us working together could bring about a miracle. I'm sure of it."

Signor Botticelli fingered one of my curls again. "Or you could stay shut up in that inferno where no one will ever see your hair or know the true color of your lips."

He was trying to work on me by giving me an alternative that wasn't really an alternative. I couldn't go back; I would be caught. He'd said as much earlier. But the truth was, happy as I was in my new good fortune, part of me didn't trust it. I distrusted all fortune I couldn't fashion with my own hands.

"I see how it is," Father Alberto said, nodding his head. "Flora, all those times you came to me in the confessional. You never let me finish. Let me finish now. *Ego te absolvo.* You have imposed a worse penance on yourself than I ever could have devised. And we mustn't forget all your good works. You were dutiful and kind to your nonna. You saved the life of your enemy at great personal expense to yourself. You saved your lackwit of a sister. And without you, there would have been no one to remember Giuliano's son. No, Flora. You need flagellate yourself no more."

I accepted his absolution, he married us, and Emilio and I left to start our new life together in Milan.

☙❧

Amore per sempre. Love. Forever. Those words sounded strange at first as Emilio situated me in front of him on his horse. I bid him say the words again, so he did. This time they landed easier on my ears, like the softest velvet. He wrapped his arms around me to grip the reins, and I leaned back into his embrace. It wasn't difficult at all.

Signor Botticelli sent us on our way with a basket of flowers for me to distribute as I saw fit. "Whether they know it or not, the people of our town need to see you. It's been a long, hard winter." Then he kissed my hand. "Now go, you two. Make merry. You have earned it."

He was smiling but seemed a little sad at our parting. It seemed fitting somehow. He used to complain about how my sister was not beautiful without her tinge of sadness. I wanted to tell him that his sadness made him beautiful as well. With his sad smile at last I understood what kind of man he was: the kind of man who could bring about a miracle, rejoice in a wedding, but cry at a parting. He may have been a genius, but he was one of us.

We stopped first at the goldsmith's, where I thanked my master and mistress and promised to write. Maria cried outright. "I never hoped to see you happy," she said. I garlanded her with daisies.

Maestro Orazio handed me a present of my old tools. "In case you get tired of being a sissy, eh?" he said with a wink. I forgave him his infrequent slaps. He had sheltered me all those years at great personal risk. Maria was right: I was no longer a debt to them.

As we left the shop and Emilio hoisted me once again up onto our horse, I looked up toward Signor Valentini's office. There were two profiles staring down at me. I waved at them. Signor Valentini waved grandly. I waited and stared at the other man with him, waiting for a gesture that would send Emilio and me to the Bargello forever. After a moment, he brought his fingers up to his face and blew me a kiss goodbye.

I handed three roses to Signor Butternut and asked him to keep one for himself and pass two on to his masters. Signor Butternut and the other guards stared at me open-mouthed. "Who are you?" he finally asked.

Emilio had already spurred the horse halfway down the street. "Today? I am the goddess of spring. *Ciao, signori!*"

Then we rode north past the *duomo* Santa Maria del Fiore and the Gates of Paradise on the baptistery doors for what was probably the last time. People stopped and stared at us as we made our progress through the streets.

Emilio called out, "What do you think of my wife, eh? Is she not the most beautiful bride you have ever seen?"

And I played my part, smiling and scattering flowers along the way. "Here, *signor*. Have a daisy." I watched closed faces of my neighbors open and they waved us on, wishing us luck. Like me, they had been through a long winter.

Our next stop was the hillside in Fiesole where there were now two graves. One had a wooden cross marked ALESSANDRA, and the second, CENESTA.

Emilio had brought Nonna's body here to lie next to his sister's. "It seemed right," he said. "This way they can both watch over us."

I want to say that on that day I felt Nonna's presence, but the truth was I didn't. I didn't need it. She had already moved on but she left a piece of herself behind in me. I still tend it as I would a rare and elegant plant — an orange tree, for example.

Our final stop before riding for Milan was the convent, where we met Domenica herself, still beautiful but faded and sad like the Venus in Signor Botticelli's painting. We invited her to come with us. We told her that Emilio had power in the duke's court, and that we could find her a husband. Maybe not one as handsome as Captain Umberto, but one who would at least treat her with respect. "Your choice," I said.

She looked first to Emilio and then to me with a look I

recognized only too well: she was jealous enough to dump my hairbrushes down the chamberpots and spit in my soup. At least she knew what she was feeling (I never did) and said she needed more time to contemplate our kind offer. "I like it here," she said. "The nuns leave me alone." I send for her yearly; yearly she refuses. I will keep inviting her until she arrives.

～❦～

And that is the end of my story. I've kept it locked up tight in a secret compartment of my heart. But then yesterday something happened that caused me to dump those memories out and sift through them like flawed gems.

We were here at our country house, everyone but your father, who was forced to stay at court to advise the duke on an important matter of state (probably the construction of another statue — I swear Barbarossa can be helpless as a child).

You, my children — Andrea, Cenesta, Giuliano, and little Alessandra — were out playing in the yard. I was pruning the roses when I heard a *thump!* I ran to the base of a tree where Alessandra lay crumpled and screaming, her arm broken so badly her bone poked through skin. I sent for the village doctor, who took one look at her and announced the arm had to come off. He even produced a saw still caked with blood from his last patient, then seemed surprised when my boot connected with his arse and sent him flying down the stairs and out of the house.

That was when I learned that memory can be stored in

our hands as well as our minds. Signor Botticelli told me I possessed my Nonna's spirit, but until yesterday I didn't think I possessed any of her talents. You all have seen how well I cook. *Madonna!* I can't stand preparing pheasants or eels. Even after I cook them they still slither down the gullet.

But standing over Alessandra as she screamed so loud I was sure the Mother of God herself heard, I found that I inherited more of Nonna than just her spirit. My hands didn't falter as I ground your sister a sedative of poppy seeds and water, set the bone straight and true, then sewed the skin shut over it.

Later, after I had hushed her down with lullabies, I came to the kitchen to see the rest of you, worry making you jump like fleas. No matter how often I assured you that her arm will heal, that next spring she will be chasing the rest of you through the garden again, you were not comforted. At first I didn't understand. After all: it was just a broken arm. Not as though she'd been pulled apart by horses.

But later, after you were all asleep, I finally understood. To you this is paradise — like the garden in my father's *palazzo* — but better since it is surrounded by rolling hills of grape vines, sunflowers, and olive trees, instead of being walled in by vanity and greed. But we cannot stay in paradise, *bambini:* sooner or later everyone gets kicked out. Nonna understood this. She wanted me to be strong, as I do you.

So I went to your father's library and found rolls of vellum, to which I have committed these memories that you might peruse at your leisure. I could no longer justify hiding the past from you. I was wrong to keep you in ignorance. You should know about what came before, both the brutality and beauty.

Now I will tell you what Nonna told my papa all those years ago: we have enough. Don't listen to those in Milan who whisper that you need better dresses, more gems, and your father would be a better ruler than the duke. We do not need to sue or do battle with the Medici for the things *Il Magnifico* took from us. I know for a fact we would lose, and I cannot watch anyone else I love get torn apart.

It has been a long night. Dawn is breaking now as I finish writing this. Outside a man approaches, limping from a gash in his leg that is wrapped in filthy linen. He is a simple man and he carries a live chicken. He sits on a bench, removes his cap, and waits. I don't know how he knew to come to me for help but it makes no difference. Something in his face reminds me of Andrea. He is not Andrea (this man has two hands) but I shall treat him as if he were, and my next patient and the next, until Andrea himself comes walking up the hillside to our house. And he will come. I have felt it on the wind, which no longer pursues me like an enemy. Instead, it tickles my ear as a lover would. It whispers: freedom. It whispers: hope.

It is time for me to end this story and begin a new one.

If there is one thing you take from my experience I want it to be this: I would have you, like Signor Botticelli, look beyond the composition of people's features, and find the spirit underneath.

I do not possess Botticelli's vision, but I fancy I can see inside the four of you. I watch you chase each other through the meadow, swat ripe fruit from trees, line up on the balcony to see who can spit best in the fountain below. And I know for certain we don't love people because they're perfect. Take Nonna, for example. I loved her despite the poison and the dire warnings. *Are you sure you want to hear this?* she had said, peeling an orange in the firelight.

Yes, Nonna. I'm sure. I know it will be a pretty story after all.

Acknowledgments

It seems that every book has a bookstore behind it, and I had the good fortune to have two. I would like to thank my colleagues at the now-defunct Madison Park Books for moral support, especially Leslie Marble, who lit a candle for me in a cathedral in Rome. I would also like to thank the staff at All for Kids Books in Seattle not only for supporting me but, by example, showing me how gracious authors behave. In case you're wondering: the best ones bring chocolate.

Peggy King Anderson was a wonderful close reader of this book from start to finish and never let me slack off. Justina Chen Headley blazed the trail. Dr. Michael Weiss and crew at Northwest Asthma and Allergy not only kept me alive through the writing of this but, through weekly allergy shots, provided me with time and space to write it.

Steven Chudney, agent extraordinaire, was generous enough to take me on and hold my hand for the more perplexing parts of the publication process. At Little, Brown, Andrea Spooner invited me to the party, and Jennifer Hunt graciously allowed me to stay. *Grazie mille.*

The biggest slobberiest thank you has to go to Juan, Sofia, and Ricardo for putting up with endless nights of macaroni and cheese for dinner, and getting used to repeating themselves whenever they needed anything from me. "Huh? Sorry, babe. I didn't hear you. I was in the Renaissance." A giant smooch to you all.

The last thank you, though, has to go to Signor Andrea of Custom Italy, for ushering me around Florence, especially for getting me into the courtyard of the Pazzi Palazzo. After four hours of richly colored paintings and frescoes, not to mention red domes and bronze doors, he lamented to me about the state of Florence today, saying that it was just a shell of its former glory. I didn't understand and told him so. Florence was one of the most beautiful cities I'd ever seen. "Yes, but can you imagine what it must have been like back then?" he said.

Perhaps I can.